# Cast of Criminals

Faint, distant, eerie piano music echoed in the empty theater. Cautiously, the Hardys followed the sound.

Joe swung his flashlight in all directions, then focused on the old player piano that was playing all by itself. Inside was a heavy paper roll with holes punched in it. As the paper went around, the holes told the piano which notes to play.

"What is that tune, anyway?" Joe asked. "It reminds me of a death march."

"Let's see," Frank said, looking inside the piano.

Joe and Frank both caught their breath. Wet blotches were spattered over the heavy paper roll—bloodred blotches.

And as the paper rolled around some more, two words appeared: CALLIE'S BLOOD!

## The Hardy Boys Mystery Stories

**Available from MINSTREL Books**

THE HARDY BOYS® MYSTERY STORIES

**97**

# *The* HARDY BOYS®

## CAST OF CRIMINALS

### FRANKLIN W. DIXON

A MINSTREL® BOOK

PUBLISHED BY POCKET BOOKS

New York  London  Toronto  Sydney  Tokyo

A MINSTREL PAPERBACK *ORIGINAL*

A Minstrel Book published by
POCKET BOOKS, a division of Simon & Schuster Inc.
1230 Avenue of the Americas, New York, NY 10020

Copyright © 1989 by Simon & Schuster Inc.
Cover artwork copyright © 1989 by Paul Bachem
Produced by Mega-Books of New York, Inc.

ISBN: 0-671-66307-0

First Minstrel Books printing August 1989

10 9 8 7 6 5 4 3 2 1

# Contents

# 1 A Killing on Main Street

"EEEYAAAH!" screamed Callie Shaw, backing away from the menacing figure with the knife.

"Who'd have thought Callie had it in her?" Frank Hardy's dark eyes glowed with pride as he watched his girlfriend fight for her life.

"Who'd have thought *Chet* had it in him?" Joe Hardy whispered as his friend stabbed Callie. She crumpled to the floor while Chet laughed wildly.

Frank leapt to his feet—and began applauding loudly. Joe was right beside him, yelling, "Bravo!"

"Can she die or what?" Frank said to Joe.

Joe grinned, then whistled loudly through his teeth. "I'll bet she could make a living at dying." He winked a blue eye at his brother.

"Hey, you clowns up there!" called a voice. "Quiet!"

1

Frank and Joe stopped clapping, leaned over the polished wooden balcony railing, and looked into the darkened theater below. They could barely make out the tall, thin figure of Paul Ravenswood sitting alone in the second row of the orchestra.

"Thanks for the applause," Ravenswood said in his deep, dramatic voice. "But I have a play to direct and I want it quiet. I don't want to be here all night. Houselights, please!" he called.

An instant later, three huge crystal chandeliers lit the auditorium. The bright lights revealed the inside of the Grand Theater in all its weary majesty: rows of faded red velvet seats and plaster walls that needed painting and repairing. Still, the people of Bayport cherished their seventy-year-old theater and enjoyed the professional entertainers who performed there. The people of Bayport also loved plays like the one being rehearsed, plays put on by Bayport's own company of amateur actors, the Bayport Players.

"Everyone onstage, please!" called Ravenswood, waving his arms as if he were conducting a chorus.

Frank and Joe Hardy hurried down from their balcony seats to join their fellow actors onstage.

Frank and Joe Hardy—actors? The idea still seemed weird to them. The brothers were more used to playing their usual roles as Bayport's two hot young detectives. But Callie Shaw was the play's star, and Iola Morton, Joe's girlfriend, was a member of the backstage crew. The girls had managed to talk both brothers into playing bit parts as, of all things, police officers in the Bayport Players' summer production. Frank and Joe had also agreed to fill in as members of the backstage crew. The production was a murder mystery, a revival of a play from the 1950s called *Homecoming Nightmare*.

Paul Ravenswood paced intensely across the hardwood stage. He clearly loved playing the part of the tyrannical director. From the way he behaved in the theater, no one would have guessed he was a bookstore manager in real life. His love for the theater was so strong that he was taking time off from his job to direct the play. As he walked across the stage, he untied and retied the bulky sweater draped around his shoulders.

"Callie, I liked the way you used your hands during that scene. But . . ." Ravenswood stopped, and everyone onstage—Frank, Joe, Callie, and the other actors—held very still, waiting to hear what he was going to say.

"Callie, have you ever been stabbed to death?" he asked.

Callie giggled and shook her blond hair. "Not since I was a little kid," she joked.

Paul Ravenswood's voice changed. It became mocking and unkind. "I could tell. You were so *dainty* about dying." He practically shouted, "It *hurts*, Callie! Getting stabbed to death hurts! So

3

don't scream when the killer comes *at* you. Scream bloody murder when he's killing you!"

Callie's soft brown eyes were wide open as she nodded at the angry director.

Then Ravenswood stared at each member of the cast, one by one, until he reached Callie's murderer.

"And just what were you doing after you killed her?" The director fired his question point-blank at the tall but slightly overweight Chet.

"I was laughing," Chet said, chewing on a caramel he'd just popped in his mouth.

"Is that what that was? It sounded to me as if you were in desperate need of blowing your nose," Ravenswood said sarcastically. "What happened to the lines you were supposed to say before you killed your victim?"

"Well, I sort of forgot them again. Then I had this brilliant brainstorm. I thought of laughing. Why not make this guy a happy kind of murderer?" Chet said.

Frank and Joe looked at each other and rolled their eyes. Chet was a good friend, but he was turning out to be a bad actor. Frank waited to hear what Ravenswood would say next.

"Chet—remember this. It's much more important to make me a 'happy kind of' director," Ravenswood shouted. "That means you learn your lines—which you haven't done—and you do absolutely everything I tell you to do. And don't think! I'll do the thinking for everyone here!"

"No sweat, Mr. Ravenswood," Chet said. "I can handle it."

"Can he?" Ravenswood turned to Frank and Joe.

"Sure. He'll nail his lines eventually," Joe said positively. "It just takes him a little longer to learn things. He didn't walk until he was seven."

Everyone laughed at Joe's joke, including Chet. Even Paul Ravenswood relaxed a little.

"Okay—" he started to say, but one of the other actors interrupted him.

"You've got to understand there's something special about Neal, your character," Raleigh Faust told Chet. Faust was the forty-five-year-old actor playing Callie's father. "Neal looks like a teenager," Raleigh went on, "but only his body has grown up. His mind is still four years old. All of his emotions explode. He doesn't just get angry. He gets *ANGRY!*"

Paul Ravenswood crossed his arms on his chest and scowled at Raleigh Faust. "Raleigh, we all know that many years ago, before most of us were born, you were the first actor to play the role Chet is trying to play. But—"

"I was just trying to help," Faust said.

"I'll take out a newspaper ad when I need help," Ravenswood snapped. "Let's try the scene

5

again. And this time, I want to hear the homecoming queen scream, and *not* hear the murderer laugh!"

"Excuse me, Mr. Ravenswood," called a voice from the back of the auditorium.

Paul Ravenswood swung around toward the empty rows of seats to glare at his young production assistant. Lyla Spring was a senior at Bayport High. She had auditioned for Callie's part, but she had had to settle for the role of the director's right hand instead.

If the Bayport Players were a machine, Lyla Spring was the grease. She did twenty jobs around the theater, and she did them all efficiently, without a complaint. As a reward, Ravenswood treated her a little bit better than he treated everyone else—but not much.

"Mr. Ravenswood," Lyla said. "A gentleman wants to see you."

"Take a five-minute break, people!" Ravenswood called, throwing up his hands.

As the cast members scattered across the stage, a middle-aged man walked down the theater aisle and approached the director.

"Well, that isn't exactly accurate," the man said to Ravenswood. "Actually I need a word with a Miss Callie Shaw. Is she here?"

Callie and Iola were standing off to one side of the stage with Chet, Frank, and Joe. Callie's head

6

turned when she heard her name, and she stepped forward. "I'm Callie Shaw," she said.

Frank and Joe instinctively followed Callie toward the edge of the stage.

"Good luck and timing. Isn't that the true secret of the world?" said the soft-spoken man, laughing lightly. He came closer to the stage, leaned on it with his elbows, and looked up at Callie. "I'm glad to see you. You're going to save my life."

The man wore an old-style suit, the kind that was popular in the 1940s. Weird, Frank Hardy thought. This guy looks like he's wearing a costume or something. A moment later, Frank found out how right he'd been.

"I'm Harry Hill," said the man. "I own the Hill Costume Supply Company. You were there yesterday, weren't you? I saw your name on the store's list."

Callie smiled brightly. "Yes, I was there renting costumes for the cast," she said.

"Well, that's my problem," said Harry Hill. "It's about the queen's diamond tiara you bought."

"You bought a tiara?" said Paul Ravenswood, interrupting the conversation. "Callie, I told you only to *rent* one. We can't afford to buy all the costumes, costume jewelry, and props for our shows."

Callie's cheeks turned a faint shade of pink, a sure sign that she was embarrassed.

"I knew you'd say that," she explained. "But I found the perfect tiara. I wanted to keep it after the play, as a souvenir. So I used my own money and bought it."

"I can understand how you feel, but that doesn't make my problem go away," said Harry Hill. "You see, I've got a customer in New York, a longtime customer, and I promised her that tiara. My clerk yesterday was new on the job—he shouldn't have sold it to you. I'll give you your money back. And I'll also replace it with another tiara—one that costs about twice as much."

Harry Hill picked up a box from one of the seats and took out a tiara. Everyone stared because it looked so real. The pieces of cut glass caught the lights in the theater, sparkling into the eyes of Frank and Joe Hardy.

"Sure, fine," Paul Ravenswood said quickly. "Now, is it all right with the world if we continue our rehearsal? Or has everyone forgotten that opening night is six days away?"

"It's not all right," Callie said quickly.

All eyes turned to her.

"I don't want to give back the tiara I bought," she said.

Joe poked his brother in the side. "What's with her?" he asked, getting only a puzzled look in reply.

"Mr. Hill," Callie explained, "when I was in your shop yesterday and put the tiara on, I com-

8

pletely forgot that I was Callie Shaw. It made me really feel like Diane, the homecoming queen in this play. I can't play the part without it."

An awkward silence followed. Harry Hill looked at Paul Ravenswood. Ravenswood looked at Callie.

"If the tiara makes you feel like Diane, keep it. Settled. Done," said the director, turning his back on Harry Hill. "Let's rehearse!"

"I hate to be a nuisance," Harry Hill said, "but I gave my word about that tiara. Tell you what—give me back the tiara, and all the costumes you rent from me come at a fifty-percent discount."

Paul Ravenswood turned around quickly. "Fifty percent?" he asked.

Harry Hill nodded twice. "To make it sweeter, let's make it for the next two years."

Everyone looked at Callie.

"I feel like I'm on a TV game show," she said, giving Frank a what-do-I-do? look.

Paul Ravenswood stepped forward and stood beside Harry Hill. "Callie." He glared up at her. "Think of the Bayport Players. We could put on an extra play next season with costumes at half price."

Callie looked totally miserable, trying to make up her mind. When she spoke, her eyes were glued to the floor. "Okay. You can have the tiara. I'll get it from the dressing room."

"Good," Paul Ravenswood said.

In silence Callie crossed the stage toward the

9

wings, with Iola in tow. Frank and Joe stood with everyone else, waiting for the uncomfortable moment to be over. Frank wanted to say, "Hey, Callie, don't let Ravenswood bully you." But he knew better than to tell Callie what to do. She made up her own mind—always had, always would.

Several minutes passed and Paul Ravenswood began to look impatient.

"I wonder what's keeping her?" Joe said softly to his brother. "She's been gone a long time."

Just then Callie walked back into the wings. "Frank?" she called. "Could you and Joe come here a minute, please?"

"What's wrong?" Frank asked, as he came up beside Callie.

Callie's face was grim. "The tiara's gone!"

# 2 Play It Again

"Come on! Iola's standing guard," Callie said, and hurried down the narrow hallway to the dressing rooms. Frank and Joe followed her.

The corridor was lighted by bare bulbs in old, molded plaster wall sockets set too far apart to provide much light. When the Hardys turned a corner and entered the women's dressing room, the change was almost blinding. Makeup tables lined the walls, each with a mirror ringed by small bright light bulbs.

Callie, ahead of Frank, shot a questioning look at Iola. Iola shook her head no.

"I haven't found it," she told Frank and Joe.

"Stupid question, but where did you leave it?" Joe asked Callie.

"It was in my tote bag," Callie said. "And I put my bag right there." She pointed to her dressing table, which was covered with a jumble of makeup

11

jars and pencils. Her open tote bag sat on top of the dressing table, with all of its contents spilled out.

"Hey, I'm not surprised you can't find something in that mess," Joe said. "Have you considered calling in a wrecking crew?"

"Maybe you left the tiara at home," Frank said, mentally running through all of the logical explanations.

"I don't forget things," Callie said.

"True," Frank agreed.

"And it was right here, in my tote bag," Callie went on. "You saw it, didn't you, Iola?"

Iola Morton was busy looking in a mirror and brushing her hair. She rested the back of the brush on her chin as she thought for a second. "You know, Callie, I got busy with operating the lights backstage. I know I came in here at some point, and I saw your tote bag sitting there wide open. But I don't remember seeing the tiara."

"Let me read your mind, older brother," Joe said. "Instant-replay time?"

Frank smiled. "Right. Let's retrace your steps, Callie," he said. "Where did you have the tiara before you brought it to the theater?"

"It was on the dresser in my room," Callie said. "I put the tiara on a teddy bear to see how it would look. Then I took a shower and got ready to come to rehearsal. I was in my room till I heard Iola's car horn beep, and then I ran downstairs."

12

"With the tiara?" Joe asked.

"In my tote bag," Callie repeated for the third time.

Frank, Joe, and Iola stared so hard at her that Callie began to look unsure.

"At least I thought I'd put it in there," she said slowly. "When Iola came to pick me up, I got halfway to her car and my dad called me back in to tell me he and Mom were going to a party tonight. They won't be home till late. Then we drove off."

"Still sounds to me like you could have left the tiara at home," Frank said.

"I really don't think so." Callie shook her head.

Finally the four teenagers went back onstage to tell Paul Ravenswood and Harry Hill about the tiara.

"The tiara's not here," Callie said.

Harry Hill's face twitched unhappily.

"Well, you've got to find it," Paul Ravenswood said. "We have a chance to save a bundle of money on our costumes, and that's no small thing." He gave the cast a withering look. "Especially when you consider how this play seems to be turning out."

"We think the tiara's at Callie's house," Frank said.

Callie squinted at Frank. She still didn't look convinced about that, but she didn't disagree.

"Hey, I'm easy," Harry Hill said in a friendly voice. "There's no law that says you have to find it

13

right this minute. Just run the tiara over to my shop tomorrow. My offer still stands."

"She'll find it," Paul Ravenswood promised, looking at Callie, not Harry Hill.

"That's fine." Harry Hill shook hands with Paul Ravenswood and left the theater.

"You know," Joe said, eager for action. "Frank and I could jump in our van, drive over to Callie's house, and be back with the tiara before the rehearsal is over."

"The rehearsal *is* over," Paul Ravenswood announced angrily.

"Oh, no. Too bad," Chet Morton said, but he sounded totally relieved.

"Except for *you*." Ravenswood pointed an accusing finger at Chet. "*You* are going to stay here and run through your lines until you murder the victim and not the script. The rest of you—I expect the mystery of the missing tiara to be solved by tomorrow so we can resume work on this play first thing. Thank you." With that, Ravenswood marched back to his seat and began making notes on his script.

"Tell Mom and Dad I'll be late coming home," Chet Morton told his sister unhappily.

"I'll tell them to rent your room," Iola answered. Then to show her brother she was only joking, she flashed him a smile as she, Callie, Frank, and Joe left the theater.

14

"You're giving Chet a pretty hard time," Joe told Iola as they walked toward their cars.

"I told him not to try out for this play. He can't act at all. But he had to be in it because you guys were," Iola said.

"You're just upset because of the way he got the part," Frank said.

"Huh?" Joe looked over at his brother. "I haven't heard this story."

"Chet told Paul Ravenswood that he knew what went through a killer's mind because he had a kid sister," Frank said.

Joe and Callie both laughed.

"Typical Chet," Joe said, still chuckling.

Joe rode in Iola's car and Frank led the way to Callie's home in the Hardys' van. When they arrived at Callie's a few minutes later, the house was empty.

"My parents must have left for their party early," Callie said as she opened the door. Once inside she ran upstairs to look for the tiara. She came down empty-handed.

"The tiara's not in my room," she said, looking pleased. "I *told* you—I took it with me to the theater."

"Did you and Iola make any stops on the way?" Joe asked.

"Tons of them," Callie said. "We had to pick up Chet and drop off the dry cleaning—"

"Too bad it wasn't the other way around," Iola joked.

"Hey! Give the guy a break," Frank said. "He's our best friend."

"Where else, Callie?" Joe asked.

"Come on—I'll show you," she answered. "If I know you guys, it's retrace-my-steps time again. Right?"

Frank nodded, and they all piled into the Hardys' van. Joe drove and Iola sat next to him, giving directions.

"We stopped at the dry cleaner's first," she said.

"Forget that. They're closed," Joe said.

"And I didn't get out of the car anyway," Callie said.

Joe passed the dry cleaner's and kept going.

A couple of blocks later, Iola said, "Stop! We picked up Chet here. He was waiting for us on that corner."

"I didn't get out of the car here, either," Callie said.

But Joe had already hopped out of the van and was rummaging through a trash can on the corner. There wasn't anything even remotely like a tiara in there. Just newspapers, soda cans, and garbage from people's lunches.

Finally Joe got back behind the wheel of the van.

"Then we drove to Burger Bonanza, the Ice-Cream Kid, and Potatoes Iz Us to get some dinner

16

for the cast. Then we drove to the theater," Iola said.

"In what order?" asked Frank.

"Gee, Frank," Iola teased. "You're the detective. Can't you figure it out?"

Frank and Joe thought for a minute.

"The Ice-Cream Kid must have been first," Joe said. "So what if the milk shakes get warm? It's worse if the food gets cold."

"Right," Frank agreed. "And you went to Burger Bonanza next. Potatoes Iz Us was last—because cold french fries taste about as good as a rubber ball."

Iola applauded and smiled at both Hardys as Joe pulled the van into the parking lot outside the Ice-Cream Kid. She and Callie hopped out and began searching the lot. Meanwhile Frank and Joe walked into the ice-cream shop. When they got to the front of the line, they were greeted with a loud, "What'll it be, jerks?"

"Just what we need," Joe muttered, "Jeffrey LeBeque." Jeffrey's goal in life was to become the most annoying, unpopular human being at Bayport High. As far as Frank and Joe Hardy were concerned, Jeffrey had achieved his goal years ago.

"Well? What flavor do you want?" Jeffrey demanded.

"Diamond," Joe said. "We're looking for a tiara. It looks like it's made of diamonds but the stones are fake," Joe said.

17

"Is it yours?" Jeffrey asked. "I'll bet you look great in it. Think about getting a lace veil to go with it."

Joe's temper hit a fast boil. "If you want to see your dentist tomorrow, Jeffrey, just keep up the jokes," he snarled.

Jeffrey backed away from the counter.

"Chill out," Frank suggested, pushing his brother behind him. "Look, LeBeque, this is a yes or no question, that's all. Did Callie Shaw leave a tiara in here earlier tonight?"

"She was in but she didn't leave anything behind," Jeffrey said.

"Thanks, Jeffrey," said Joe. "You ought to try out for the football team. We could use a new tackling dummy."

From inside the van Callie and Iola watched the Hardys walk toward them empty-handed. "We didn't find it, either," Callie said as Frank sat beside her.

Joe climbed behind the wheel and asked no one in particular, "How did Jeffrey LeBeque get a job where people come to eat?"

"His father got it for him," Callie answered.

"But his dad owns the competition—Scoops du Jour," said Joe.

"That's why he got Jeffrey a job at the Ice-Cream Kid," Iola explained.

The stops at Burger Bonanza and Potatoes Iz Us

were just as unsuccessful. No one at either place had seen Callie's lost tiara.

It was nearly midnight by the time Joe stopped the van in front of Callie's darkened house.

"My mom and dad still aren't home," Callie said. "You guys want to come in for a frozen pizza and watch some TV?"

"Sure," Frank said quickly. He could tell Callie didn't want to be alone.

She unlocked the front door and stepped into the dark living room. "Hold it a sec while I get the lights," she said.

Callie started to walk across the living room, but Frank suddenly grabbed her shoulder and pulled her back onto the porch. "I hear something inside," he whispered.

Joe listened, too. "Yeah—someone's in there. Are you sure your parents aren't home?"

Before Callie could answer, a loud crash came from somewhere in the house!

# 3 A Thief in the Night

Frank and Joe quickly stepped into the dark living room, motioning Callie and Iola to stay outside. Joe kept his fists and muscles tensed, ready to fight.

Joe strode forward, hit his shin on a low coffee table, and went sprawling. The next instant, he heard footsteps coming down the stairs. In the dimness he saw someone rush into the living room, heading for the front door! As Joe scrambled to his feet he saw Frank grapple with the figure. Then he saw the intruder shove Frank down. Frank's head hit the coffee table. The intruder was getting away!

Joe lunged and tackled the figure easily around the ankles. But the intruder squirmed out of Joe's hold and got up again quickly. They were near the front door now. Out of the corner of his eye Joe saw another figure coming toward him. Were there two intruders?

As Joe jumped to his feet he bumped into the second figure and knocked it down. Then he heard Callie's voice saying, "Ouch, sorry."

The intruder had seen Callie coming, too. Now he suddenly changed directions, heading for the back of the house. Frank and Joe pursued, running through the dining room toward the kitchen. But they stopped outside the kitchen. It was strangely quiet. Had the intruder already left? Or was he hiding, waiting for them? They crept into the kitchen softly and looked around. Empty.

The Hardys knew there were two back doors to Callie's house. One was in the family room, which was off the kitchen to the left. The other was in the kitchen itself and led to the garage. Joe held up two fingers for Frank to see in the moonlight. Then he split the two fingers apart—a signal to separate.

Frank nodded and went toward the door to the garage. Joe went to the left, down two small steps to the family room. Slowly, carefully, Joe opened the sliding glass doors and stepped out. His toe caught the edge of a clay pot sitting on the patio just outside the door. It was dark on this side of the house—no moonlight. Was anyone on the patio? In the yard? No, Joe decided. All was quiet. He was alone.

As he stepped back into the house, Joe heard a

floorboard creak. His heart started pounding. Someone was in the family room with him. Yes! Over there on the other side of the couch. Joe held his breath. Then, with a shout, he leapt through the air.

If this is Frank, I'm going to pound him anyway, Joe thought. I signaled him to go to the garage. An instant later, Joe's shoulder connected with the other person in the room and they both went down. Joe knew immediately that the figure he'd landed on wasn't Frank. He had tackled his brother enough times in their lives to know that.

This guy's smaller than Frank, a real lightweight, Joe thought. But the intruder was strong. As Joe struggled with him, the thief slammed his fist into Joe's stomach. Joe doubled over, and the burglar took off.

Joe straightened and lunged after the figure, who darted ahead through the still-dark house. Joe rounded a corner into the kitchen and— SMACK! He ran headfirst into Frank.

"Watch it!" Frank yelled. "He's getting away!" Together the brothers dashed back to the living room, taking the same route the intruder had. By now the living room lights were on so it was easy to see the room was empty. They ran outside, but the intruder was gone.

Frank rubbed his sore head and stared at his brother in frustration.

"Well, it looks like we lost him. Hey, where are

the girls?" Frank wondered, suddenly looking around.

Joe didn't have to answer because, right then, both girls appeared at the front door.

"I heard someone out on the patio," Callie explained. "Iola and I went around the house to investigate, but no one was there."

"That was me," Joe said with an embarrassed grin. "I kicked a flowerpot."

"Sorry about running into you in the living room," Callie said. "I was trying to get to the light switch. It's halfway across the room." She pointed to the far wall, so Frank and Joe could see what she meant. "Mom hates that thing because we can never see when we come home at night."

"Did you get a look at the burglar?" Frank asked both girls.

Callie shook her head. "He must have run out the front while we were in the back," she said, "because we heard some tree branches snapping. Then we heard what sounded like a motorcycle start up and take off."

"Yeah, I heard that, too," Frank said. "It sounds like a hot engine. About four-fifty cc."

"What did the thief want?" Callie asked, her voice suddenly shaky. Now that the whole thing was over, she was starting to get scared.

Frank and Joe shrugged at the question.

"The tiara?" Iola asked softly.

"I don't think so," Frank said. "It doesn't make

23

sense. If the tiara is missing because someone stole it from Callie's tote bag, they wouldn't try to steal it again. They've already got it. And if the tiara's missing because Callie lost it somewhere, then no one stole it and this is an unrelated incident. And there's only one way to find out what the burglar was after."

So the four friends explored the house room by room, turning on lights and checking for damage and any missing items. Nothing was missing from downstairs, but in the den they found a window that had been slid wide open. Joe stretched a lamp on its cord to bring some light to the window.

"The lock's been broken," he said, picking up a piece of window hardware from the rug.

Frank ran his hand along the windowsill and pointed out deep gouges in the paint and wood. "Whoever broke in used a crowbar," he said.

"But what did he want?" Callie asked again.

"Maybe we'll find the answer upstairs," Joe said.

Callie climbed the stairs slowly, not too eager to see what was awaiting them. At first, the bedrooms looked as untouched as the rest of the house. Then they got to Callie's room.

"Oh, no!" she cried out when she saw the mess. Her room looked as if it had been plundered by Attila the Hun on one of his angrier rampages. Everything from her closets had been pulled out and tossed in the middle of the floor. Drawers had been taken out of chests and turned upside down. Even the sheets had been ripped from the bed, and the mattress was crooked on the box spring. Callie, in shock, stared at the destruction in her room.

"What kind of slime would do this?" Iola asked no one in particular. "I mean, it's weird. He tore Callie's room to pieces and didn't touch anything else in the house."

"It's not weird," Frank said quickly. "It's a clue."

"What's it mean?" Iola asked.

"This guy's not a regular burglar," Frank said. "Pros always go straight for the master bedroom. This guy was looking for something special, maybe something he knew was here."

Callie just walked around the room looking totally freaked out. Then she began picking up her jewelry, which was lying in a heap on the floor, and putting it back in her jewelry box. "But I don't see anything missing," she said. "Nothing. It's all just a big mess. Maybe the thief was looking for the tiara."

"Let's go downstairs and talk," Joe said. "We'll figure this out—as soon as I get something to eat."

While Joe, Iola, and Callie microwaved a pizza, Frank prowled around the living room. A few minutes later, he came into the kitchen with a smile on his face and his fist closed around something.

"What did you find?" Callie asked eagerly. "Did the burglar drop his wallet or something?"

Instead of answering, Frank slapped his palm down on the counter. When he lifted his hand away, a brown tortoiseshell shirt button lay on the counter.

"Recognize it, Callie?" Frank asked.

Callie stared at the button carefully, then shook her head.

"Great," Frank said, putting the button in his jeans pocket. "I'll bet it's the burglar's. He must have lost it in the fight."

"My brother is a human vacuum cleaner when it comes to clues," Joe said proudly. "He just gets down there and swoops them up, even when you don't think they're there."

Frank grabbed a piece of pizza and started walking toward the kitchen. In between bites, he puzzled out the case with Joe. "Okay. Let's talk about what we know about this guy," he said. "He's thin, and he looked like he was shorter than you, Joe."

"He wears blue jeans and sneakers," Joe said. "They felt like high-tops when I grabbed his feet."

"He spends money on clothes," Callie offered.

"How do you know that?" Joe asked.

"They don't put tortoiseshell buttons on cheap

26

T-shirts," Callie answered with a confident tilt of her head as she tugged on Joe's T-shirt.

Frank smiled at Callie.

"And he rides a motorcycle," Iola reminded them.

"You know when I said he wasn't a regular burglar?" Frank said. "I think I'm changing my mind. Even though he didn't take anything, this guy seems like a pro. He's really careful about what he does. He shows up with the right equipment, searches the right room, and even when we showed up, he didn't panic. He doesn't make mistakes."

"Stop it, Frank," Callie said. "You're making me scared again. It feels like he's still here."

"Hey, worry not, Callie," Joe said, popping the top on a soda can. "We're here, too. And we'll stay till your parents come home, so there's nothing to worry about."

*Rinnnnggg!*

"It's probably my parents, saying they're still at the party," she said.

"Ask them to come home," said Frank. "But tell them there's nothing to worry about."

Callie walked over and picked up the cordless phone from its base. Quickly she extended its antenna.

"Hello?" she said.

"Speaking."

Callie went pale. "What? What did—"

"Hello? Hello?"

Callie's hand, still holding the telephone, dropped by her side.

"Who was it?" Frank asked.

"I don't know." Callie had a terrified look on her face. "All the voice said was, 'If you want to be safe, Callie Shaw, you'd better stay out of the play.'"

# 4 Another Case

Callie dropped the portable phone on the counter with a clunk and sat down with her friends. Her pale skin turned even paler, making her eyes stand out like large brown buttons.

"Was it a man or woman?" Frank asked.

Callie shrugged. Her eyes were glassy as she relived the brief but frightening conversation. "Man, I think. I don't know."

"Why not?" asked Iola.

"I couldn't understand what he was saying at first. He didn't even sound human."

"Maybe he had his hand or something else over the phone to muffle the sound," Joe said.

Frank said, "Tell us again what the voice said."

"It sounded like 'Stay out of the play,'" Callie said. "But, it could have been 'Stay out of the way.' I wanted him to repeat it but—"

"But he hung up fast," Joe said, finishing the

sentence. "He's smart. He wasn't taking any chances about you remembering his voice." Joe angrily crushed a soda can in his hand.

"What's going on?" Callie asked. "First my tiara is stolen at the theater. Then someone breaks into my house. Now this weird phone call."

"I think someone's trying to scare you out of the play," Frank said, putting an arm around Callie's shoulder.

"Well, he's got a snowball's chance in July if he thinks he can," Callie said firmly. "Nothing's going to stop me from playing Diane."

Frank smiled, but his voice was serious. "We'd all better keep our eyes open."

Iola and the Hardys were still with Callie when her parents got home at one-thirty. They all explained to Mr. and Mrs. Shaw what had happened while they were out. In the end Callie's parents agreed with Frank and Joe that the intruder probably had been someone playing a cruel prank. Still, although nothing had been stolen, Callie's parents decided to report the break-in to the police.

By the time Frank and Joe got home and hit their beds, it was almost three in the morning. So when the phone rang later that morning at seven-thirty, neither of them wanted to answer it. Frank finally grabbed the phone because he knew his parents liked to sleep late on Sundays, too.

30

"Hi, Frank." Frank didn't recognize the girl's voice at first. "Mr. Ravenswood wants you and your brother to come in early today. Can you be here by nine?"

"Oh . . ." Frank said, recognizing the caller. It was Lyla Spring, Paul Ravenswood's production assistant. "Right," he said sleepily, "nine tonight. See you then."

"No—nine this morning," Lyla said so seriously that Frank laughed.

"I know. Just kidding, Lyla," Frank said. Then he hung up the phone.

Frank and Joe entered the Grand Theater through the rear door. No one was backstage so they headed out front. As soon as they walked onstage, Paul Ravenswood called to them. He was pacing the carpeted aisle behind the last row of seats in the auditorium.

"Hello. Lyla says you two really are detectives." Ravenswood's voice boomed in the emptiness.

"We've solved a few," Frank said.

"I can't hear you. Project," scolded the director.

"Yeah, we're terrific," Joe called. Joe Hardy didn't have a lot of patience, and he was losing it all when it came to Ravenswood.

"I guess I should have asked you last night to find the missing tiara, shouldn't I?" the director said.

31

"We're looking for it," Frank said. "It wasn't in Callie's house."

The director pulled on the arms of the sweater that was draped around his neck. "While you're at it, do me a favor and figure out who broke into this theater last night."

Broke into the theater? This was news to Frank and Joe. The Hardys looked at each other with a what's-going-on-here? question in their eyes. First the tiara, then the break-in at Callie's house, then the phone call, and now this. Were these four separate, unrelated events? Or were they connected somehow?

"What happened?" Frank asked the director, who was still pacing at the back of the theater.

"Can't you see?" Ravenswood swept his arm broadly. Then he marched down the aisle and climbed up on the stage to show them the evidence firsthand.

"Look at this," he said, walking over to an old stuffed chair. The fabric had been torn to shreds and the stuffing pulled out. Then he showed them a sofa that also had been ripped apart. Backstage, he showed them storage chests, prop trunks, and wardrobe racks that had all been vandalized.

"Was anything stolen?" Frank asked when they were again standing on the stage.

"Stolen? Isn't this enough damage for you?" Ravenswood roared. His voice sounded like thunder.

Joe didn't answer Ravenswood's question. Instead he asked one of his own. "How'd the vandals get in?"

The director's voice returned to normal. "The front door," he said.

Joe and Frank jumped off the stage and hurried down the aisle to the lobby of the theater. They examined the front door. The simple lock had been pried open with something that gouged and split open the wooden door frame. Two deep indentations showed where a tool had been used.

"Crowbar," Frank said.

"Right," Joe agreed. He got down on his knees to get a good look at the gouges. "And look at this. There are some slivers of green paint deep in these dents."

"Green paint? Callie's windows are painted green," Frank said.

"I know," Joe said. "It has to be the same crowbar—and the same guy using it." Joe stood up and stuffed his hands into his back pockets. He and Frank walked back to Paul Ravenswood.

"Well?" asked the director.

"Well, we know who did it," Frank said.

Ravenswood's eyes widened. "You guys *are* fast!" he said admiringly.

"It was the same guy who tore up Callie's house last night," Joe explained.

"What's his name?" Ravenswood demanded impatiently.

33

"We don't know yet," Joe admitted.

"But we're going to get on it right now," Frank said.

"Good," Ravenswood said. "But let me remind you, I still expect you to do the work you promised to do around here. Show up for every rehearsal. We have a saying in the theater—The show must go on. So find this creep for me, but do it on your own time, *puh-lease.*"

Frank and Joe just shook their heads at Paul Ravenswood's behavior. Had he really gotten them out of bed at seven-thirty on a Sunday morning to ask them to find the missing tiara and solve a break-in on their own time? The guy was a star in the nerve department.

But so what, Frank decided. Ravenswood's attitude didn't really change anything. He and Joe were working on the tiara case already. And if the break-in at the theater provided more clues—all the better.

The Hardys had a quick private conference and decided that the best place to start their investigation was in the theater itself. Maybe they'd find another button—or some other lead to the identity of the guy with the crowbar. Before they got busy cleaning up the mess the vandal had made backstage, Frank and Joe advised Ravenswood not to report the vandalism to the police.

"Nothing was stolen and you want to get on with rehearsals, don't you?" Frank asked.

The director looked shocked. "Of course, of course. No police," he said, and walked away.

Meanwhile the other actors and crews began to arrive by ones and twos. As soon as everyone was present, Paul Ravenswood quickly got the rehearsal going. He started with a scene between Chet Morton, Raleigh Faust, and Amelia McGillis, the red-haired actress playing Callie's stepmother in the play. In the scene Chet's character, Neal, comes to pick up Diane, played by Callie, to take her to the homecoming dance.

"Good evening, Mr. and Mrs. Thorne," Chet began. "I've been looking forward to taking Diane to the homecoming dance all week."

Throughout the scene Chet bit his nails; he cracked his knuckles; he cleared his throat.

Raleigh Faust, playing Mr. Thorne, had an annoyed look on his face. He was no longer acting. "No, no, no. It's all wrong," he burst out. "Can't you see that? You just don't understand what Neal is all about. You're acting as if you've already killed the girl. You've got to be cool, calm, and collected."

Chet looked from Faust to Ravenswood and back again. "But Mr. Ravenswood told me yesterday to let my inner turmoil show through."

Faust rolled his eyes. "Paul, may I remind you that when I played the part, I was directed by the man who *wrote* this play. I think he knew how the part of Neal should be played."

35

"Raleigh, you can remind me all day, if you like," Paul Ravenswood shouted back. "But you're not in charge here!"

Amelia McGillis clapped her hands to her ears. "Oh, great. Here we go again."

"I will make this announcement one last time for everyone in the cast. If you need to, go outside and read the sign in front of the theater. You'll see that *I'm* directing this play. So keep your comments to yourselves."

"So I was doing it okay?" asked Chet. "How was my inner turmoil, Mr. R.?"

"Were you doing it okay?" Paul Ravenswood asked himself. "Were you doing it okay?" he repeated in a louder voice. "Were you doing it okay?" Ravenswood shouted as he stepped up onto one of the seats in the auditorium. "Let me put it this way, Chet. I've seen *chef's salads* with more inner turmoil! You weren't acting as if your soul were in agony. You were acting like someone whose shirt collar was too tight!"

"I don't get it. Do you want me to take my shirt off, Mr. R.?" asked Chet.

"Would you possibly come to pick up your date for the homecoming dance without a shirt on?" Paul Ravenswood demanded.

Joe Hardy, working offstage with Frank, couldn't resist. "Chet would!" Joe shouted.

Everyone laughed, except Paul Ravenswood. He

36

waved his hands in front of him as if he were erasing Chet off a blackboard. "I want to try a different scene," he demanded. "Act three, scene two."

That was Joe's cue for a set change. Quickly he carried out a cushioned chair that Frank had hastily repaired and set it in the middle of the stage.

"More downstage," called the director tensely.

Joe moved the chair closer to the front.

"Stage left," Paul Ravenswood said. "No—too much."

Everything had to be perfect—that is, the way Ravenswood wanted it. Finally the director told Callie to come onstage and sit in the chair.

The theater grew quiet. Callie sat in the chair, framed in a spotlight. She pulled her feet up under her on the cushions. Her character in the play was supposed to be thinking about all the things that were frightening her—the threatening phone calls, the other girl who had been murdered in the very same dormitory, in the very same room, during the homecoming dance ten years before. Callie began breathing harder, nervously pulling her hair back. Fear mixed with anger and bewilderment flashed on her face. She rolled herself into a tighter ball and suddenly gripped the arms of the stuffed chair.

"Kill me!" The words exploded from Callie's

heart. "Go ahead and kill me right now, if that's what you want. I know you've been planning it, so just go ahead and do it—now!"

Then Callie jumped to her feet. "Pretty good," said Paul Ravenswood calmly from his orchestra seat.

An instant later, before anyone else spoke, or moved, an enormous heavy gray wall crashed onto the stage—smashing the chair where Callie Shaw had been sitting just five seconds before!

# 5 Curtains?

Frank and Joe watched in horror from the wings as the enormous gray wall fell from above. When its bottom edge hit the stage, the entire theater shook. Callie fell to her knees.

"Callie!" Frank yelled, and raced onstage. The wall was so enormous that even though Callie had not been sitting in the chair, she'd still been close enough to be hurt.

Before Frank reached Callie someone was already helping her up—a gray-haired man in coveralls. Frank recognized Ernie, the stage manager and janitor for the Grand Theater. "She's okay," Ernie said to Frank.

Shaking like a leaf, Callie was a strange kind of okay. Her eyes searched the group of people crowding around her. When she saw Frank, she tried to smile.

Frank smiled back, then asked. "What was

that?" He looked to the experienced theater people for an answer.

"Fire curtain," Raleigh Faust answered.

"Who lowered that curtain? What's going on?" Paul Ravenswood screamed as he charged onto the stage.

"Nobody lowered it," Ernie said. "The fire curtain just fell."

"Curtain?" said Joe. "What kind of curtain makes that kind of noise?"

"A fire curtain," Ernie said, pointing to the enormous gray thing that had fallen. "It's a thick, fireproof curtain—weighs about a ton with the chains on the bottom. In the old days, when there was a fire backstage, we'd drop the fire curtain to keep the fire from spreading. The curtain hangs in the fly space." He pointed straight up.

Frank and Joe had been around the Bayport Players long enough to know that the fly space is the space, two stories high, above the stage. Painted backdrops, called flats, and other pieces of scenery are hung or "flown" up there, and are raised or lowered by ropes during scenery changes.

"The fire curtain is not supposed to come crashing down and ruin my rehearsal!" Paul Ravenswood acted as if the accident had happened to him, instead of Callie. "It's supposed to be doubly secured up there."

"I'm going to check," Joe said softly to Frank.

He walked over to a metal ladder that went straight up the back wall of the theater and began climbing.

At the top of the ladder, at least one story above the stage, were catwalks, long narrow walkways just wide enough for one person. Joe understood why the shaky structures were called catwalks as he crossed the rafters. You needed the sure footing of a cat *and* nine lives to fool around up there, he thought, stepping carefully.

Frank wanted to keep an eye on his brother, but he had his own work to do. He suspected that the fire curtain hadn't fallen by accident. And if it wasn't an accident, he thought, then I want to know who saw what just before that curtain crashed down.

Asking witnesses what they'd seen was an old trick of their father's. Fenton Hardy was a veteran police officer turned private detective, and he often gave Frank and Joe some inside tricks of the trade.

"When something happens, don't ask people where they were," Fenton had explained to his sons. "That makes people nervous. Instead, ask everyone what they saw—and who they saw. Pretty soon, if you're lucky, you find out that there was someone nobody saw. That's your main suspect."

Frank walked back onstage. Most of the performers were milling around, waiting for direc-

41

tions from Ravenswood. Frank pulled Chet aside. "I need your help," he said. "Who and what did you see right before the fire curtain fell?"

"I saw angels," Chet said. "They were all wearing hip boots and they were singing."

"What are you talking about?" Frank asked.

"After Ravenswood as much as told me to get lost, I went backstage. I was catching some Zs," Chet admitted. "Next thing I knew, there was this tremendous crash. It woke me up. Are you and Joe making a case or something out of this?"

"A case?" Frank said. "You must still be dreaming, Chet."

Next, Frank questioned Raleigh Faust, but that didn't go anywhere, either. Faust had been playing cards with Ernie in the wings opposite where the Hardys were standing. Faust and Ernie both saw Callie, but not much else.

"I saw Paul, of course," Faust said archly. "Playing the king from the second-row seat."

Frank left Faust and walked over to Iola. He knew where she'd been—as the production's lighting technician, Iola had been controlling the lights. But what had she seen?

"I saw my brother sleeping with his mouth open," Iola said. "And I saw the curtain fall. Before that I saw you and Joe in the opposite wings. Not much help, huh? Sorry, Frank."

So Frank went off to look for Lyla Spring. He

found her in the small, windowless manager's office at the back of the theater. She was seated at a battered wooden desk, piled with stacks of paperwork. Only one thing gleamed in the dim and dusty office. The shining object, an eight-by-ten-inch silver frame, held the photograph of a girl. Frank knew immediately who it was—Lyla's older sister, Deirdre.

Lyla sat motionless, the eraser tip of a pencil touching her lower lip. She was staring at the photo.

"Thinking about Deirdre?" Frank asked softly.

Lyla jumped. She turned quickly in the creaky swivel chair and gave Frank an angry look that melted quickly. "You scared me."

"Sorry," Frank said, "but I've got to ask you some questions about what just happened onstage. Did you see the curtain fall?"

Lyla nodded her head. "That's why I came in here—once I saw Callie was okay. It really shook me up." She smiled. "But I'm glad you and Joe are investigating," she said. "I know you'll find something out. The same guy who broke into the theater last night dropped the fire curtain, don't you think?"

"Maybe. But I'm not sure how."

"Poor Callie. She's really getting it," Lyla said. "Do you think this guy's looking for something or just wants to scare Callie?"

43

"Hey, let me ask the questions, okay?" Frank laughed. "Who did you see out there, right before the curtain fell?"

"You mean, who *didn't* I see?" Lyla said. "I know how you Hardys work. You think I forgot how you and Joe jumped into action when Deirdre ran away—even when the cops told you to lay off?"

"I wish we'd found her, Lyla," Frank said. "We tried."

Lyla nodded. "That was two years ago." She was quiet, thinking. "Amelia. I didn't see Amelia McGillis when the fire curtain came down."

"Thanks," Frank said. "I'll ask her where she was."

He turned around and bumped right into Joe.

"Frank, I found something up there," Joe lowered his voice as they walked down the hall. "I checked out the fire curtain rope—cut, all the way through."

Frank's face tightened. That could only mean one thing. "The rope was cut by someone here in the theater—just an instant before the curtain fell!"

"Right," Joe said. "And in the commotion, whoever cut it had plenty of time to climb back down the ladder and blend in with the crowd."

"Come on," Frank said. "Lyla may have given us a lead."

The Hardys practically ran to the women's

44

dressing room. Frank knocked, and the unlatched door swung open. Inside, Amelia McGillis, with her back to them, was packing a tote bag. She turned her head as the door opened.

"Hi, darlings," she said, continuing to stuff makeup and costumes into her tote bag.

"Where are you going, Miss McGillis?" Frank asked.

"Darling," Amelia McGillis said, walking over to Frank and putting a soft hand on his shoulder, "yours truly is checking out of this loony bin."

"Why?" Frank asked.

"Because the play's jinxed. It's trouble," she replied.

"Miss McGillis, where were you when the fire curtain fell?" Joe asked.

"Yours truly was in her dressing room, taking a little snooze. Beauty sleep, I call it. And it's a good thing or I might be dead. Do you know what that curtain weighs?"

"Did anyone see you?" Frank asked, ignoring her question.

The actress shrugged. "Who cares? No one's going to see me leave, either."

"You're just walking out? What about the motto of the theater—the show must go on?" asked Frank.

Amelia McGillis laughed harshly. "Darling, do you know what's going to happen soon? Right now Raleigh and Paul are just arguing. In another day, they'll start shooting at each other. I've done enough shows with both of them—it's bad enough when we're getting paid at the local dinner theater. But when they do a show for the Bayport Players, for *art,* they really become nut rolls. Now add in the costume tiara disappearing, the theater being broken into and vandalized, and an actress almost being squashed by the fire curtain. I don't have to consult my horoscope to know it's time to hustle out of this play. I'm not getting paid for this, you know."

Just then Paul Ravenswood appeared in the dressing room doorway. He looked at the stuffed tote bag and at Amelia McGillis. Then he rushed over to the dressing table and grabbed a long makeup brush. "Go ahead, Amelia. Thrust it into my heart. That's what you're doing. If you leave this production, I'm dead. Can you do this to me, Amelia? Can you do this to yourself? And can you walk away from the performance of your life?"

Frank and Joe didn't know whether to applaud or not. What an act Ravenswood was putting on!

Tears sprang into Amelia McGillis's eyes, and she ran toward Paul Ravenswood with open arms. "I'm sorry, Paul," she said. "I'll stay."

"Good. I want you onstage in fifteen seconds!" he snapped as he passed through the doorway.

Amelia McGillis ran to keep up with him, leaving Frank and Joe staring at each other.

"I think Amelia told the truth about one thing," Joe said. "They're all nut rolls."

"Maybe. And maybe some of them are just *acting*," Frank said.

Back onstage the Hardys found everyone huddled around Paul Ravenswood. He was speaking in an unusually soft voice so that cast and crew had to listen very carefully to hear every word.

"The police have been summoned about the unexplained occurrence in this theater. They will do their job. A repair crew has been summoned to lift and rehang the fire curtain in the fly space. They will do *their* job."

He sounded like a patient teacher.

"And now I expect you to do *your* job. That is, to act. The show opens on Friday. That's in five days! This show must go on, and it will go on, and it will go on if it kills us!" he said. Then he ordered everyone to return at noon the next day for a full rehearsal.

When Callie, Amelia McGillis, Chet, and Raleigh Faust took their places onstage the next day, they were all in optimistic moods.

"From now on, everything's going to go smoothly," Callie said positively.

"Yeah—I'm not going to be a laughing killer anymore. I promise, Mr. R.," Chet said.

"All right, people. I am extremely happy to hear

47

that," Ravenswood said. "Now, please take your places for the dinner scene."

"Dinner scene?" Joe said. "That's my cue. I've got to crank up the old fogger. See you later."

Quickly, and as quietly as he could, Joe pushed the artificial-fog generator across the stage in back of the scenery. He placed the machine behind a piece of scenery that contained two French doors.

Onstage, the dinner scene began. Frank watched from the wings.

Callie, playing Diane Thorne, sat at a table with her stage parents, Raleigh Faust and Amelia McGillis. Neal was there too, played by Chet.

"Delicious dinner, Mrs. Thorne," Chet said.

"Chet, that line is not in the script," Paul Ravenswood called from the darkened auditorium.

"Just being polite," Chet said.

"Well, *don't* be polite!" Paul yelled.

"Okay," Chet said. He opened his mouth and belched loudly.

"Just say what's in the script!" Ravenswood yelled. "Start again, please."

"It's a cold and foggy night," said Faust. "I hope you kids won't have any trouble driving to the homecoming dance."

Faust looked at Chet. Callie looked at Chet. Amelia McGillis looked at Chet. There was a deathly silence in the theater.

"Who me? Is it my turn? Line, please." Chet

turned to Lyla, who was standing in the wings with the script.

"I will not tolerate this!" The director jumped to his feet. "Chet Morton, you're fired!"

Chet stood up so fast his chair fell backward. "Fine. I'm out of here. I'm not sticking around another minute."

"That's thirty seconds too long!" the angry director shouted back as Chet stomped offstage. Ravenswood sighed. "Let's take a lunch break, everyone. And, Lyla? This afternoon we start auditioning for the role of the killer."

Kneeling behind the piece of scenery, Joe heard everything. Oh, no, he thought. Just when I've gotten this monster ready. "Mr. Ravenswood," Joe yelled.

Peering through the French doors, Joe could see the director looking around, trying to locate the voice. Joe stood up and waved, then pushed open the French doors. "Don't call lunch now. I'm all set to show you the fog machine."

The director almost smiled. "You mean something will actually work around here?"

"Guaranteed. You're going to love it, too."

Paul Ravenswood sighed. "We'll see," he said. "Callie, let's do just the fog scene before lunch."

Callie quickly took her place upstage center. She stood in front of the French doors.

"I need fresh air!" Callie flung open both doors

and stepped outside. "The night feels clammy, like a wet wool glove." Callie's voice could be heard in the farthest seats of the theater. Clouds of thick white fog seemed to roll toward her.

"Why do I feel like someone is watching me?" Callie said, deeply inhaling the fog, which had started to pour through the door. "Why—"

Suddenly Callie stopped speaking and clutched her throat. Coughing, choking violently, she gasped for air!

# 6 The Killer Mist

"The fog," Callie gasped, stumbling around the stage, trying to get away from the thick cloud. The mist puffing from the machine backstage swallowed her up.

"Relax, Callie," Paul Ravenswood called from the seats. "Those old foggers always give off a little smell. You'll get used to it."

"Here's an old remedy." Raleigh Faust hurried onstage, carrying a ceramic mug. "Hot water, with honey to coat the throat. It works—"

The mug fell out of his hand, splattering hot water all over the stage. Faust doubled over, coughing and choking, too.

"Something's wrong," Faust gasped, lurching backward away from Callie.

Frank jumped into the thick white blanket and pulled Callie offstage. "Turn off the fog machine,"

51

he shouted to Joe, behind the set. "Someone open the front doors!"

Frank, hardly breathing, ran across the stage through the fog again. He had to get to the opposite side of the theater to reach the backstage door. Frank propped open the door to start the air circulating and blow the fog out of the theater.

By now, the fog had rolled into the seats. Paul Ravenswood got a deep breath of it and instantly added his voice to the chorus of chokes and hacks. "Joe Hardy, what did you put in that fogger!"

Joe, coughing himself, had removed the cover from the machine's water tank. He bent over and smelled immediately that a chemical no one would mistake for perfume had been added to the water in the tank.

That did it—more sabotage! Joe hurried onstage. He saw Frank standing just offstage, but before he could say anything, a voice called out from the back of the theater.

"How's it going?" Harry Hill strolled slowly down the center aisle toward the stage. Wearing another 1940s suit, he was a walking advertisement for his costume shop.

I wonder if he ever wears a gorilla suit, Joe thought.

The thick cloud of fumes had begun to flow away, so Harry was smiling instead of coughing. "Thought I'd pick up the tiara myself," he said.

The missing tiara—Joe had forgotten all about

52

it. Years seemed to have passed since he, Frank, and the girls had looked for the tiara.

From the wings, Callie stepped downstage and cleared her throat. Her eyes were tearing. "Mr. Hill, I can't find it," she said.

"Oh?" He stretched out the word. "Have you looked very, very hard?"

Callie's forehead wrinkled. "I've looked everywhere," she said. "I'm sorry. I just don't know what could have happened to it."

"I guess you don't," Hill said. "But that doesn't put the tiara in my hands." He looked at everybody onstage. "Look, old customers are very important to me. So I'm going to up the ante. If the tiara is returned within twenty-four hours, I will give the Bayport Players *free* costumes for the next twelve months."

Someone let out a surprised whistle—Paul Ravenswood. He looked as if he might start jumping up and down like an excited kid at a birthday party.

He motioned with his long fingers for Lyla Spring to step forward. "Lyla, I want you to *find the tiara*. We can't leave it to these amateur detectives, can we?"

Lyla looked a little confused. "But what about getting someone to replace Chet Morton? You said nothing was more important than that."

"Do both," Ravenswood answered, already turning his back on Lyla. "Without fail."

At six that evening, after pushing all the actors hard and driving Lyla crazy, Ravenswood finally called an end to the rehearsal. Everyone left quickly except Frank and Joe, who told Ravenswood they were staying late to fix the sets.

The truth was, the Hardys wanted the old theater to themselves.

"What should we look for first?" Joe asked. "The knife that cut the fire curtain rope? Or the stuff that was poured into the fog machine?"

"The tiara," Frank said.

"I don't get it," said Joe. "You want to look for the one thing we know *isn't* here?"

"Right." Frank nodded. "Harry Hill came to get that tiara himself—not once but twice. Why? That's a job for a delivery guy."

Frank walked across the stage toward the dressing rooms. Joe followed him.

"I want to find out if that tiara was ever here," Frank said.

"Ever here?" Joe asked.

"Sure. If we can prove that it *was* here, then we'll know that Callie didn't misplace it. We'll know it was stolen, maybe by the same person who keeps doing a number on this play."

They started going over the women's dressing room thoroughly, as if they had never been there before. Frank checked for signs of forced entry— gouges, scratches, pried-open drawers or doors.

Joe looked for even more obscure clues, like a

54

sliver of silver paint, or maybe a piece of glass from the tiara's phony gems. They needed something that would prove to them the tiara had been in that room.

After covering every inch of the floor, Joe took a miniflashlight from his jeans and checked the floor of the dressing room's small closet.

"Hey," he said quietly.

It wasn't what Joe said but the way he said it that made Frank stop. He knew Joe had found something good.

"What?" Frank asked, walking over to his brother.

Joe was on his knees in the small closet. He didn't answer with words. He knocked on the back wall of the closet and produced a hollow thud. Next he punched the wall hard near the floorboards. A thin nail gave way, and the wallboard toppled forward.

"Whoa," Frank said. "It's a phony wall."

"I knew it when I saw the light from my flashlight shining through the cracks," Joe said. He leaned forward, aiming his light into the opening.

"What's in there?"

"Nothing special," Joe said. "Just dust, cobwebs, and some old stairs."

"Stairs?" Frank said. He gave his brother a push. "Let's go."

First Joe and then Frank squeezed through the

narrow opening in the back of the small closet. Behind the opening was an empty hallway. Joe's flashlight beam danced off the large sticky spiderwebs on the walls and near the ceiling.

"It's a whole other part of the theater," Joe said. "I remember Ravenswood said that half the theater had been closed up to save on heating bills. The upstairs dressing rooms, he said. This must lead there."

"I'll bet no one's been in here for twenty years," Frank said.

The Hardys climbed the stairs, making little explosions of dust under their shoes as they stepped on the creaking wood. At the top, they came to a large room, another dressing room, with makeup mirrors, tables, and chairs. Everything was covered with dust.

"Pretty neat. It looks like a dressing room for ghosts," Joe said.

"This area was probably sealed off years ago when they remodeled the theater," Frank said, walking around the room.

A 1962 calendar hung on a nail in the wall. Old jars of makeup and several hairbrushes still sat on the tables.

"Hey," Joe said, turning toward the door. "I heard something."

They both listened.

"A mouse?" Frank suggested.

"Think you can come up with something wimpier?" Joe laughed.

"How about the wind?" Frank said.

They both laughed.

"Let's just check out what else is up here." Joe nodded toward another door at the far end of the hallway.

That door led into another narrow hallway with doors lining both sides. Frank and Joe started opening them. Some rooms seemed to be offices. Another was a rehearsal room with an old piano. One room had old cots with no mattresses.

Joe froze and flashed the light behind him. "I heard it again," he said. "It was a squeak."

"I told you it was a mouse," Frank said.

"Uh-uh. A squeak like sneakers make on wood." Frank grinned. "Okay—a mouse wearing running shoes."

*Slam!* A door down the hall closed loudly. For the Hardys, the sound was like a starter's gun. They raced down the hallway toward the door—to find it locked tight!

Joe jerked the handle roughly. "Congratulations. We've just walked into someone's trap," he said angrily.

"Maybe," Frank said. "But if there's another way down, we'd better find it fast before it gets locked, too."

They split up. What had started out as an

exploration to satisfy their curiosity had turned into a save-our-hides mission. Find a room, find a stair, find a ladder. It didn't matter what. It all added up to the same thing—find a way out.

Frank opened every door as he went back down the hall. Closet. Office. Bathroom. An old telephone booth—minus the telephone. None of the rooms had windows, none of them led anywhere. By the time Frank came back to where he'd left Joe, his hair and clothes were coated with dust.

"Hey, Frank," Joe called. "You look like you rolled down the hall."

"You don't look much better, fuzz ball," Frank said. "Find anything? I didn't."

Joe snapped his fingers. "I knew there was something I wanted to tell you," he said. "How does a rope sound to you?"

"Old-fashioned but it'll do," Frank said with a smile.

Joe led his brother to what had obviously been a storage room for props and costumes. All kinds of dusty old stage props lay on the floor, everything from fireplugs to dueling swords. Behind a curtained wall, Joe had found a window. It looked down onto the stage from two stories up. And in the corner of the room was a coiled rope.

"We tie the rope to something," Joe said, "drop it out the window, climb down—and hope the rope holds till we reach the floor."

"It's worth a shot." Frank looked around for

something to tie the rope to and spotted a heavy wooden desk.

He and Joe secured the rope to the desk and dropped the end over the windowsills.

"Ready?" Frank asked. Joe nodded, gripped the rope, and stepped out the window.

"Take it slow," Frank cautioned.

"Yeah, I know," Joe said. "Too fast, and I'm a puddle on the floor. Anyway, I've got to be careful. You'd never solve this case without me."

Frank watched Joe's smile dip lower and lower, below the window.

The rope swung back and forth under Joe's shifting weight. But it hugged the wall, so Joe quickly got into a rhythm of letting the rope help him walk down the wall. He'd take a step, let a little of the rope slide through his hands, hold on, then take another step. It was slow going—and worse, the old rope was crumbling in his hands.

Joe felt the rope tear a little. His body slipped down, just half an inch. When he looked up, he saw that a rotten section was starting to come apart.

"How far to go?" Frank called down to him.

"Don't know. Can't see. And the rope is giving out," Joe said.

Seconds later Frank heard his brother yell.

Seconds after that, Frank heard the thump of a body hitting the wooden stage. "Joe!" Frank called. "Joe!"

There was no answer. Then a shaky voice called, "I'm okay. The rope broke."

Joe had suddenly fallen about eight feet—and he didn't land standing up. It took him a few moments to get up and make sure nothing was broken.

"Hang tight, Frank. I'm coming up the old stairway to let you out," Joe yelled.

Joe's thigh was sore, and his hands hurt from scraping along the brick wall during the fall. But he hobbled toward the women's dressing room and climbed the hidden stairs behind the closet to free his brother.

"You really okay?" Frank asked as soon as Joe unlocked the door.

"Yeah. Let's get out of here," Joe replied.

The two brothers turned and headed down the stairway. Suddenly, Frank stopped.

Faint, distant, eerie piano music was echoing in the supposedly empty theater.

Who was there? And where was the music coming from?

Cautiously, the Hardys followed the sound.

"If this is some kind of a joke, I'm not laughing," Joe said. The music echoed loudly now, filling the theater. But no piano was in sight.

"It's coming from over there." Frank pointed across the stage. Against the wall in the wings opposite were a pile of wooden crates and furniture. Frank followed the music to the wall and

60

found a tarp covering one large rectangular shape. He jerked the tarp away to reveal a piano.

Joe swung his flashlight in all directions, then focused again on the upright piano that was playing all by itself. It was an old player piano—the kind that had two sliding doors on the front above the keys. Behind the doors was a heavy paper roll with holes punched in it. As the paper went around, the holes told the piano which notes to play. Most old player pianos had to be pumped by foot to make them work. This one apparently had been fitted with an electric motor so it would play by itself.

"Who turned that thing on?" Joe asked.

The two brothers stared at the piano as it played an old-fashioned melody on its out-of-tune strings.

"I'd guess the same guy who locked us upstairs," Frank said.

"Well, he has lousy taste in music," Joe joked. "What is that tune, anyway? It reminds me of a death march."

"Let's see." Frank slid open the two doors, then caught his breath. Wet blotches were spattered over the heavy paper roll—bloodred blotches.

As the paper rolled around some more, two words appeared: CALLIE'S BLOOD!

# 7 Sour Notes

The piano kept pounding its out-of-tune music while Joe searched for a switch to turn it off. Every few seconds, the bloody words scrawled across the piano roll's heavy paper appeared, then rolled down out of sight. CALLIE'S BLOOD.

In frustration, Frank finally stopped the music by yanking the piano's electrical cord out of the wall socket. Silence.

The silence lasted only a second. It was broken by the slam of the heavy stage door at the back of the building. The sound rang through the entire theater. Hearing it, the Hardys knew that whoever else had been in the theater with them had just left. Callie's unknown enemy had knocked off for the night. But what was he planning for tomorrow?

Frank ripped the music roll out of the piano and crunched it into a ball. "I don't get it. Callie never hurt anyone," he said.

Joe shook his head in angry confusion.

"Don't tell Callie about this, okay?" Frank told his brother.

"No problem. She's had her tiara ripped off, her house broken into, the fire curtain dropped on her, and nearly got gassed by the fog machine." Joe ticked off the events on his fingers. "Even as tough as Callie is, learning about this would put her over the edge. But it makes you think, Frank. Going out with a girl like that could be hazardous to your health."

"Very funny." Frank smiled. "Let's go. I want to talk to Dad about all this."

Back home, Frank and Joe found their parents in the den with their aunt Gertrude, looking at pictures the boys' aunt had taken on her recent trip to Arizona.

"The star actors!" Aunt Gertrude said, when she saw Frank and Joe. "Are you doing Shakespeare, boys?"

"Our play is a little newer, Aunt Gertrude," said Joe.

"And we're not the stars," Frank said.

"I'm sure you're just being modest," Aunt Gertrude said. "I can't wait to see your debut."

"Hey, Dad," said Frank, "we've got to show you something on our van."

"It's getting dark out, guys," said Fenton Hardy. "Show me in the morning."

Frank rolled his eyes. Great, he thought. Dad

can find a clue, but he can't take a hint. "How about making us one of your world-famous black-and-white sundaes, Dad?" asked Joe.

"Sorry, pal. We finished the ice cream yesterday," said their father.

"Fenton, snap out of it," said Aunt Gertrude. "Can't you see the boys want you to go and discuss one of those mysterious cases that you never discourage them from getting involved with?"

Fenton Hardy cleared his throat with some embarrassment. "Oh. Right. Well, I'll give them a good scolding, Gertrude," he said with a wink as he followed his sons into the kitchen.

"Anything left from dinner, Dad?" asked Joe.

"Do a little detective work on your own," his father suggested, pointing to the refrigerator. "So what's up. What are you guys working on?"

While Joe made a couple of what he called Empire State Building sandwiches—the sandwiches his mother said he needed a building permit to construct—Frank told his father the details of what had been going on at the theater. He told him about what had happened to Callie, about the false wall of the closet, about Joe and him being trapped, and about finding the player piano and its bloodred message.

"Amelia McGillis, the actress who's playing Callie's stepmother, says the production is jinxed," Frank said. "She even—"

Fenton Hardy stopped Frank right there.

"Amelia McGillis?" he said. He was thoughtful for a long moment before he went on. "Guys, I'm sorry to say this, but that name doesn't just ring a bell. It sets off an alarm."

"What for?" asked Joe.

"This goes back a lot of years, when I was just starting out on my own. I got a security assignment from a shopping mall that was having a major shoplifting problem. I staked the place out, and the short of it is that Amelia McGillis was the problem."

"You arrested her for shoplifting?" Frank said, thinking immediately of Callie's stolen tiara.

"It was more complicated than that," said Fenton Hardy. "She wasn't just a thief. She couldn't stop herself. Her need to steal was a disease."

"You mean she was a kleptomaniac?" asked Joe, shoving his hand into a bag of potato chips.

His father nodded. "She promised to get professional help and to pay the stores back for everything she'd taken. So I arranged for charges to be dropped and hushed the story up. I didn't see any reason to ruin her young life. She kept her promise, and ever since then, the only time I see her name is when she's acting in a local play. I hope you'll be very careful with this information, guys. Don't jump to any conclusions."

Frank and Joe nodded. But they couldn't help feeling that they were finally getting the break in the case that they needed. Their father's memory was like glue. And this time the glue helped stick an important piece together for Frank and Joe. It was time to question Amelia McGillis.

"Thanks, Dad," Joe said, scooping up the rest of his sandwich and heading for the back door. "That's going to give us a lot to talk to Miss McGillis about. Will you get a move on, Frank? You drive. I'm still eating."

"Business as usual," Frank said with a laugh.

Amelia McGillis lived by herself in the smallest house on Cady Falls Road. It was a pretty street during the day, but it took on a different personality at night. Large trees cast strange, moving shadows on the houses and lawns.

Frank and Joe parked their van under a dim streetlight and then crunched up the short stone driveway. Standing on the porch of the dimly lit house, they could hear a television playing inside.

Amelia McGillis answered the doorbell wearing blue jeans and a sweatshirt with *A Chorus Line* across the front. "Hi, darlings," she said, looking at the Hardys through the screen door. But she didn't smile the way she usually did, and she didn't try to act years younger, either. "I guess I should have kept the porch light burning for you two."

"What do you mean?" asked Frank.

She opened the door with a sigh. "It means I've

been expecting you. How's your old man? Is he still a primo straight-arrow guy?"

"Yeah, that's Dad," Joe said.

Amelia McGillis motioned the boys in, and they followed her into the living room. The room looked tired, as though it wanted to catch up on its sleep for a while. The couch and chairs sagged and needed new fabric. The rug had some holes. On the mantel over the fireplace was a double row of printed programs, glass-framed, from the regional plays Amelia McGillis had been in. She moved quickly to a low coffee table and pushed some spread-out sheets of paper into a stack that was still not too neat. Then she very deliberately put the stack under a large ashtray on the table—as if she wanted the papers out of sight. "I've been rehearsing my lines," she said.

Her eyes darted from one brother to the other, and Frank thought she seemed a little nervous.

"Your father told you about my sticky fingers, didn't he?" She waggled her long-fingered hands in the air.

Frank and Joe nodded.

She crossed her arms over her chest and sat down on the arm of the couch with a sigh.

"That was a long time ago, darling," Amelia McGillis said, shaking her head. "I was young and beautiful then, as young—and almost as beautiful —as Callie. But I was different. I needed things."

She uncrossed her arms and held her hands tightly in her lap. "I don't know why I needed things. But I did. When I'd see something in a store, or in someone's house, I didn't just want it. I *had* to have it. Something just came over me." She extended her arm, looking at her hand as if she were modeling an expensive ring. "I liked jewelry best —and I took it." She dropped her hands to her side and stared at the two brothers. "That's all *finito*—done with. It has been for years."

She stood up and walked over to the mantel where the glass-framed theater programs were arranged. There were also photographs of her as a young actress. She stared at a picture of herself wistfully.

"You use the same dressing room that Callie uses, don't you?" Frank asked.

Amelia McGillis turned to face them, her eyes narrowed as she nodded.

"Did you ever see the tiara? Maybe you noticed it in Callie's tote bag?" Frank asked.

"Never," Amelia McGillis said loudly. "I didn't know Callie had a tiara. I never saw it. *I don't take things anymore.* I don't even steal scenes!" She finished her sentence with a joyless laugh.

Just then the telephone rang in another room, and Amelia McGillis went to answer it.

Frank and Joe immediately looked toward the coffee table. They both wondered why the actress would hide a copy of the script.

68

"Go see if that call's a wrong number," Frank said.

A wrong number would mean she'd be back before they could do any investigating.

Joe tiptoed to the door of the living room and listened.

"So, how's it going, hon?" he heard Amelia McGillis say cheerily.

Joe tiptoed back. "It's okay!" he said. "Sounds like she's talking to a friend."

Joe quickly lifted the ashtray while Frank pulled the pages out from underneath.

"It is a copy of the script," Frank said. "I was sure she was trying to hide something." He began to flip through the script, looking for something suspicious.

But in the next instant, Frank was snapped back to reality by the sound of a low cough.

Amelia McGillis! He and Joe had completely forgotten to listen for her coming back.

The Hardys' heads spun toward the sound.

Amelia McGillis stood in the doorway. Gripped in her hands—her long-fingered hands, which had captured the brothers' attention before—was a gleaming, sharp-looking butcher's knife!

# 8 Too Many Knives

The Hardys instinctively jumped back, away from the coffee table.

A strange look came over Amelia McGillis's face. "So you've found me out," she said. Her voice suddenly sounded totally different—cold, determined, and cruel.

Joe, recovering first, stepped forward calmly, confidently. "Come on. Give me the knife, Amelia." It was casual-Joe talking, best-friend Joe, who didn't want anything to happen to Amelia.

Now Frank started to move slowly toward Amelia McGillis from the other side.

"Hey, if you've got problems," Joe said easily, "let's talk about them."

Suddenly Amelia McGillis began to shriek hysterically with laughter. "Oh, darlings," she said. "Oh, darlings," she repeated as she lowered the knife.

"Your faces look like two plates of mashed

70

potatoes. Don't tell me I really wound your clocks with that little gag?" She howled. "Guys! I came in to ask if you wanted a sandwich! I buy unsliced bread." She waved the knife. "When I saw your reaction to this, I couldn't resist performing." She laughed again.

Frank and Joe didn't join her. They didn't think what she'd done was funny. And they didn't know whether she was telling the truth or not.

There was nothing much the Hardys could do. So they said good night awkwardly, got in the van, and headed home. Joe drummed his fingers nervously on the steering wheel as he drove. Frank sat in grim silence.

"Okay," Joe said, "two plus two is four, fish gotta swim, birds gotta fly, and actors can be weirdos. Those are the facts. The question is—is Amelia responsible for what's been happening to Callie?"

Frank shifted uncomfortably in his seat. "Callie's tiara's been stolen, and Amelia's a kleptomaniac. Someone's just missed seriously hurting Callie twice in the last forty-eight hours, and Amelia McGillis runs around waving butcher knives for laughs. Based on that, it's kind of hard to discard Amelia as a major suspect."

"Yeah, I wanted to believe it when Dad said her problem was over. But maybe we can't. Maybe she's still sick and maybe she's really got it in for Callie for some reason."

71

"What reason?"

"Jealousy," Joe suggested. "Maybe she sees Callie as a younger version of herself. And she doesn't like being reminded that she's over the hill now."

"Could be," Frank said in a faraway voice.

"You don't sound too convinced," Joe said. "Got any other suspects?"

"Harry Hill," Frank said quickly.

Joe stopped the van with a screech. "Excuse me," he apologized. "I couldn't drive and catch that wild pitch at the same time."

"What's so wild about it?" asked Frank. "Harry Hill's awfully interested in finding that stolen tiara."

"Yeah, but getting that tiara stolen is the first thing that happened to Callie. If Hill was responsible for that, why is he coming around the theater trying to get us to find it?" Joe said.

Frank was silent. Joe's logic was right on the money. Joe started driving again.

"Now what about Harry Hill's customer?" Joe asked. "The woman in New York who wants the tiara? Sounds like she may be jumping on Hill's case with cleats."

"Why would she insist on Hill getting her the tiara if she stole it?" Frank asked.

Smack. The investigation had hit the same dead end from two different directions.

"Good question. I don't know," Joe said as he pulled into their driveway. "But maybe we'd better find out who she is."

They both agreed that that should be their next step. But it was a step that would have to wait.

First thing in the morning the next day Joe drove over to Pick of the Litter, a used furniture shop, to bring back some replacement chairs for the production. Frank bicycled to the theater alone. He'd promised to stand in at rehearsal, just reading the part of the killer, until someone was found to replace Chet. Frank arrived at the theater just as Lyla was about to go in, carrying a shopping bag.

"What's in the bag, Lyla?" he called, locking up his bike.

"Tiara!" she shouted back, slipping into the theater.

Frank smiled. Something was finally going right. He hurried into the theater. Several members of the cast and crew were gathered on the stage. Lyla was reporting to Paul Ravenswood, who stood at a table, squeezing fresh orange juice in a hand squeezer.

"Mr. Ravenswood, I found an actor to play the killer," Lyla announced proudly. "I also"—she reached into her shopping bag—"brought this." She placed a tiara on the table.

"Oooh!"

"Way to go, Lyla!"

"You did it!" Paul Ravenswood said with total surprise. "Free costumes for a year!"

"But that's not my tiara," Callie said.

Lyla looked over at Callie and nodded. "I know. I was about to explain. I haven't found yours yet, so I rented a new one."

Callie pushed the tiara away. "That's nothing like mine," she said. The strain was beginning to show—her voice was too loud. "I can't wear that. My character wouldn't wear that in a million years."

"You know," Lyla said, pulling her hair back with a jerk of her hand, "I'm getting a little sick of people dumping on me. All I'm trying to do is get this show on the boards—whatever it takes. And it would really help if I felt like I wasn't the only one who cared."

"Hey, Lyla," Frank said quietly. "You do a great job. Everybody knows that."

"Yes, of course," Paul Ravenswood said. "Now, what about the replacement actor you found?"

"Hello there!" The voice came from offstage. "I think that's my cue."

A young man walked toward the knot of people at the center of the stage. He was of medium height and lean, with coal-dark eyes. He wore a white dress shirt, sleeves rolled, and blue jeans.

Frank thought the guy was about twenty, but he

74

had the kind of soft, open, smiling face that always looked younger.

"Matt Anglim," he said, shaking hands with Paul Ravenswood.

"Not exactly a household name," said Paul. "Am I hoping for too much if I hope that you have acted before?"

Matt smiled. He seemed to enjoy the director's sarcasm, but then he hadn't lived with it as long as everyone else had.

"Right now I'm in prelaw at Bayport Community College," Matt said. "But I did some off-off-Broadway staged readings last summer. When I saw Lyla putting up flyers all over town, I said, why not? I spoke with her, and she told me to come in this morning and try out."

"Well, someone give him Chet Morton's script," Paul announced. "It was hardly used at all. Let's try act two, scene three."

Frank was pleased he wouldn't have to act as a stand-in after all. He was also curious to see how Matt would work out. So he took a seat in the dark theater to watch the rehearsal.

Callie and Matt took their places off to one side of the stage. Then the scene began. Callie, slipping comfortably back into her character in the play, recited her lines from memory. Matt read from the script, which he carried. Soon Frank and everyone else watching forgot that Matt was carrying a script at all. His voice was powerful. And his

75

words seemed to be both innocent and threatening at the same time.

"It's getting late," Callie said.

"I know," said Matt. "But it's such a beautiful night. Let's walk."

"I don't want to miss the homecoming dance," said Callie.

Matt walked around Callie, once, twice, like a spider spinning out its web around a trapped bug. "I've been looking forward to this night, too," he said. "Not just because of the dance but because I'm here with you, we're here together—and there's no one else around. I'll bet you could even scream, scream as loud as you can, and no one would hear you."

"Stop, Neal, you're scaring me," Callie said.

Then, instead of reading his next line right away, Matt stared at Callie, as though he were memorizing each angle of her face because he'd never see it again.

Frank felt goose bumps on his arms. This guy's not just good, he thought, he's sensational.

Suddenly Matt laughed. "Scaring you," he said, looking down again at his script. "That's the last thing in the world I want to do. This is homecoming night, and you're going to the dance with me and not Bob. By the way, why did you decide not to go to the dance with Bob? Did you and Bob break up?"

"I don't want to talk about Bob," Callie said.

"Because you still like him?" asked Matt.

"I don't like him. He scares me," Callie said. "I think he's gone mad."

"Why? Does he carry a knife like this?" Matt reached out toward the auditorium where Paul Ravenswood was sitting. "I'm supposed to have a knife. Where's the prop box?"

"Stage left," Paul called from the darkness.

"Don't go away. I've got to kill you now," Matt joked to Callie, and he walked to the side of the stage.

Callie smiled at Frank and gave him a thumbs-up signal about Matt, which Frank returned with a nod. Yeah—Matt was good all right. Almost too good. It gave Frank the creeps.

"Let's pick it up from 'Does he carry a knife,' okay?" Matt asked when he came back to Callie. He was carrying a prop knife. Its plastic blade was dull and mounted on a spring. When it hit any-thing, the blade slid into the plastic handle. Matt tucked the knife between his shirt and jeans, just above his left front jeans pocket. Then he cleared his throat and began reading his script. "Why? Does he carry a knife like this?" Matt whipped out the prop knife.

"Neal! What are you doing with that?" Callie asked in horror.

"The only thing one can do with a knife like this. I'm going to kill you," Matt said, raising his arm and the knife high above his head.

"Neal—no! You can't—you don't . . ." Callie turned to run, but Matt stalked her, then stabbed, driving the plastic knife toward Callie.

She screamed, falling to the floor and rolling onto her back.

For a moment, Matt Anglim stared in confusion at Callie's limp body on the floor. Then everyone watching started to applaud.

Frank couldn't believe how much better the scene had gone this time. Callie was—Frank stopped clapping. Something was wrong. Callie wasn't moving, she wasn't getting up.

"Hey!" Matt stared down at the broken knife in his hand. "I think I really stabbed her!"

# 9 A Dark and Stormy Night

The prop knife dropped from Matt Anglim's hand, clattering on the stage. "Are you okay?" he said, kneeling by Callie. Frank leapt to the stage, pushing Matt aside.

"Callie? Are you hurt? Are you okay?"

Big tears were welling up in Callie's eyes, tears of pain, fear, and anger.

"I'm okay," she gasped. "Just cut a little. Didn't expect . . . Sick of this!"

Frank picked up the prop knife, pushing its bent blade against the palm of his hand. The blade didn't slide into the handle the way it was supposed to. Someone had jammed the spring. Callie was lucky the cheap plastic had just nicked her. Anything harder and she'd have really been hurt.

"I haven't seen so many things go wrong in one

production since I was in *Mason's Zanies*," grumbled Raleigh Faust.

"Darling," Amelia McGillis said, clicking her tongue at Faust, "give us a break. It's bad luck even mentioning that play."

"Why?" asked Iola.

"Jinxed," Amelia McGillis whispered.

"Jinxed?" repeated Iola.

"Okay, okay, accidents will happen." Paul Ravenswood cut through the nervous chatter. "Matt, you say you haven't acted much before?"

Matt shook his head.

"Have you killed anyone before? You were excellent," Paul Ravenswood said.

Frank blinked. Had he really heard Paul Ravenswood use the word *excellent?*

"I disagree," Raleigh Faust said. "When I played the part of Neal on Broadway—"

"When you played the part, we were all in diapers," Paul snapped. "So just can it, okay?"

Ravenswood immediately got everyone back to work on the play, although Faust sulked for the rest of the afternoon.

This is my chance to duck out, Frank thought, and try to find out who Harry Hill's New York customer is. But Paul Ravenswood grabbed Frank before he could escape. Ravenswood sent Frank to the print shop to pick up copies of the play's poster. Joe had arrived with the new chairs when Frank got back. But before Frank had a chance to talk to his brother, Ravenswood ordered them to drive all over town putting a poster in every shop window and on every bulletin board in Bayport. Frank didn't really mind. In fact, he was proud to do publicity work for Callie. But when would they get time to really sink their teeth into this case? he wondered.

Late that night a heavy rainstorm moved through Bayport, knocking trees down and adding bright special effects to the sky. Thunder sounded like rockets passing close overhead.

Callie, Iola, Frank, and Joe could all hear the storm as they sat on the couch in Callie's family room. But their attention was focused on the television screen, where they watched a videotape Iola had made that day. She had brought her dad's camcorder to the theater to tape Callie rehearsing.

Sometimes Callie watched attentively, leaning closer to the screen, her elbows on her knees, her cheeks between her hands. Sometimes she watched with a pillow covering her face.

"I can't believe I did that," she said. "It's so stupid. Tell me when it's over."

Frank and Joe watched the videotape carefully, too, but for a different reason. They hoped to find some clue to who was terrorizing the production. It had occurred to them—not just once—that the culprit might be someone in the cast or crew.

Raleigh Faust, for instance. They didn't know much about him, but everyone could see how

81

much he and Ravenswood hated each other. The two fought constantly, especially over how to play the part of Neal, the murderer, which Faust had played so many years ago. Could Faust be the mastermind behind all of the accidents and mishaps? He had the motive—to ruin things for Ravenswood.

But where was one shred of evidence?

The videotape played on. The Hardys watched Matt stab Callie, checking for anyone who seemed too interested. They particularly watched Amelia McGillis. Lyla Spring made faces into the camera for a while, then took over as camera operator so Iola could be in the tape.

"Watch their faces," Frank said. "They get mad at each other. But no one ever gets angry with you, Callie."

"What's that mean?" Callie asked.

"It means that we've been looking for someone who wants to hurt you," Frank answered. "But maybe that's all wrong. Maybe all this person wants is to ruin the play."

Another zap of lightning flashed. The lights in the house flickered, and then went out.

"Rats," Iola said. "We were just getting to Callie's big scene. Got any candles?"

Callie stood up, then sat down again quickly between Frank and Iola.

"Relax. It's just the storm," Frank said, pointing

to the window. "See? All the lights in the neighborhood are out."

"I'm really losing it," Callie admitted. "For a second I thought somebody had cut the wires."

Thunder boomed loudly and ended with a ringing echo.

Finally Callie realized the echo was the telephone ringing. She picked up the receiver. "Hello," she said. After a few seconds, she slammed the phone down on its cradle.

"What was that?" asked Frank.

"Him again." Callie's lips were tight. "He said, 'Get out of the play. I've warned you. Next time may be your last.'"

"Oh, no," Iola said.

Joe got up in a hurry. "I'm going to find some candles and get some light in here."

"Was there anything different about his voice or the way he talked?" Frank asked. Maybe Callie had caught some kind of clue.

"Something different?" Callie said. "Yeah. I'm twice as freaked out now."

Joe came back with a lit candle, carefully shielding the delicate flame. The flickering light did something odd to Callie's face. She was beautiful —and determined—still, but the light showed dark circles around her eyes, emerging like knots of wood under a thin coat of paint.

Iola came over and tugged playfully at her

friend's arm. "Come on, Callie. Lighten up," she said, giving her friend a brave smile. "I'll bet Frank's right. It's not you personally."

"My big brother could be right," Joe said with a grin. "It's happened once or twice."

Iola saw that Callie was not convinced. "Okay. Those phone calls are for real, we've got to face that. Some slime ball probably thinks it's a great joke. But you know what I think? I think all the other stuff—the tiara, the fire curtain, the knife, the gas in the fog machine—all that could be accidents or coincidences."

"Accidents?" Callie repeated the word with a little laugh. She wasn't buying it.

"Sure. The tiara, for example," Iola said. She paced as she thought of her example. "Suppose it hasn't been stolen. You know how you always put stuff down anywhere that's close. Maybe you put your tote bag with the tiara in it down on a chair or some other piece of furniture we're using in the sets. Maybe the tiara fell out and got pushed aside or covered up."

"You mean it's still in the theater where I left it?" Callie asked.

Iola nodded.

Callie gave her friend a sad smile. "But Frank and Joe searched the theater."

Frank's head snapped around toward Callie and Iola. He was suddenly interested. "Uh-uh," he said. "We just searched the women's dressing room."

"I'd be happy to search the rest of the place—right now," Joe said. "Let's stop talking about clues and go find one."

Iola grabbed her purse and pulled out a key. "Lyla gave me this because I might have to let delivery men into the theater."

"Then let's go!" Frank said, grabbing Callie's hand.

At just past midnight they all climbed into the Hardys' van. Frank drove slowly through the downpour. The windshield wipers slip-slapped the rain on the window in a quick rhythm. After a few blocks, Frank was relieved to see streetlights and traffic lights still operating. He increased his speed and they soon arrived at the theater.

Iola unlocked the door, and they walked in, shaking the water off their windbreakers. Backstage was as dark as Callie's neighborhood had been. Iola flipped a switch. A single base bulb lit, casting a dim glow on the backstage area.

Joe moved quickly toward some furniture stacked near the stage. Then he stopped. "Hey, guys," he called softly. "We're not alone."

A light shone up from under the stage. Joe moved to the front of the stage silently. The light came from underneath a door in the orchestra pit, between the stage and the first row of seats.

"What's under there?" Joe asked Iola, who knew every room and hallway in the theater.

"Storage rooms," Iola said.

"Well, someone's down there tossing things around," Joe said, listening.

Iola called down from the edge of the stage. "Hello? Mr. Ravenswood? Is that you?" She called again because a long, loud rumble of thunder outside had covered up her voice.

No one answered. And the noise from under the stage had stopped.

With a crash, the storm outside intensified. The lights in the theater began to flicker. Was the power going to go off in this part of Bayport, too?

When no one answered Iola, Joe tried calling. "Hey, Lyla? Miss McGillis? Who's down there?"

Finally they got an answer of sorts. But not a friendly one. The light below the stage snapped out. And still no one answered.

"I don't like this," Frank said. He was the first to leap off the stage, dropping eight feet into the narrow orchestra pit. Joe was right behind him. Seconds later they had started down the dark stairs under the stage.

"There's a light switch at the bottom, on the left side," Iola called after them.

Frank reached out, feeling the wall with both hands as he led the way down the stairs.

"I can hear him running," he said quickly and

86

quietly. "Talk about good timing. I think we've nailed this phantom we've been after."

The footsteps stopped just as Frank snapped on the light. He and Joe could now look around in the sudden glare from the bare bulbs overhead. They were in a long storage room with a low ceiling. Large wooden crates, props, and set pieces lay everywhere. The person they were looking for could be behind any one of them. The two brothers walked toward a door at the end of the room, a door that led—who knew where?

Suddenly a ghostly figure leapt from behind two crates, twenty feet away from Frank and Joe.

"What is this? Halloween?" Joe yelled.

The figure was covered by a sheet that hung down to his knees. As he ran, the sheet flapped behind him.

"He's heading for the door!" Frank shouted.

The Hardys chased after him. Suddenly there was a crack of thunder so loud the building seemed to rock. The lights flickered, and died.

In the sudden, complete darkness, Joe ran right into a wooden crate.

"Yow!" he shouted when his knee collided with the wood.

"Joe? Are you all right? Where are you?" Frank called.

Seconds later, he heard a door bang open. Then the lights came back on. Frank saw Joe rubbing his knee, but the sheeted figure was nowhere in sight. The door at the end of the room was now wide open.

"I'm okay, Frank, let's go!" Joe yelled. They both bolted for the doorway, landing in a smaller, damp-smelling chamber. Then the lights went out and they were in the dark again.

"He's here somewhere," Frank said.

"Come on out, whoever you are!" taunted Joe.

In answer to Joe's mocking song, the door to the room slammed shut. Once more Frank and Joe were locked in a dark, unfamiliar part of the old theater.

"He was behind the door!" Joe shouted angrily. "When are we going to stop falling for this jerk's traps?"

"Face it. He knows this theater better than we do," said Frank. "Any idea who he is?"

"No. I didn't get any hint."

"Not with that sheet covering him. What's he up to—studying to be a mattress when he grows up?"

"Save the jokes," Frank said. "Let's find a light switch and get out of here. You go left, I'll go right."

They stretched out their arms, and moved slowly.

"I found the wall," Joe yelled.

"Good start. I'm not there yet. Do you think

Callie and Iola could hear us if we shouted?" Frank asked.

"We're right under the stage, but I'll bet this room is soundproof," Joe answered.

"That means if they scream, we won't hear them, either," Frank said grimly.

"Hey! Don't even think about that, Frank," Joe said, and started moving faster.

"Frank! Hold it. I've found a switch of some kind. Might even be an old circuit breaker. It feels like a long lever," Joe said.

"I hope it's still wired up to something," Frank said.

"Only one way to find out. Here goes."

Joe pulled the lever, but the lights didn't come on. Instead he and Frank heard a mechanical groaning, a grinding of gears above their heads. Grit dusted Frank's face, then fell in a clump on his head.

In the next instant, something even larger dropped on Frank, knocking him flat.

He lay on the cold floor, stunned for a moment, before he realized that what had hit him was—a body!

# 10 Just Dropping In

For several moments Frank couldn't move. He was pinned by the lifeless form that had fallen on him. He lay beneath it, gasping for air.

"Frank? Are you okay?" Joe called. He was coughing, his mouth was filled with dust, and he couldn't see anything in the dark room.

"Yeah." Frank wiggled out from under the body.

"What happened?"

"A body fell on me," Frank said with a shiver.

"A body? As in *dead body?*"

"You got it," said Frank.

Suddenly the body lying next to him twitched. A voice moaned.

"No!" Frank said quickly. "Apparently it's alive."

The moan came again, this time in a voice Frank recognized.

"Callie!" he shouted, and helped her up. At first she swayed and bent as if she were made of rubber, but finally she started to come around.

"What happened?" Callie asked groggily. "I was standing on the stage and then . . ."

"Where's Iola?" Joe asked.

"I don't know," Callie answered. "She left." Callie's voice was fuzzy and her words came slowly. "Someone ran at me. No lights. I grabbed him. Tried to stop him. But he hit me and I fell on the stage."

"You fell right on the trapdoor," Frank said.

"And when I pulled that lever, trying to turn on lights, the trapdoor opened and dropped Callie on your head," Joe said. He looked up. The theater was so dark he could barely see the opening in the ceiling.

"What did the guy look like?" Frank asked Callie.

"He looked like a sheet," Callie said, with a little laugh. She was starting to feel better.

"But you grappled with him. Was he tall, short, thin, fat, six arms, five legs? What?" Joe said.

"He was shorter than Joe. And he felt thin," Callie said. She began to shake. "He was about the same as the burglar who broke into my house."

"Shh," Joe said.

He'd been the first to hear it. The door to the small, damp-smelling, and now dusty chamber was being unlocked. Then it started to open.

"How's that for luck?" Joe whispered. "We get a second chance at nailing this guy."

In the dark, the two brothers crept toward the door, ready to pounce when it opened. The door creaked.

Joe leapt first at the dim figure in the doorway. He knocked it to the floor and got a scream—fear, panic, and surprise mixed into one shrill blast.

"Iola!" Joe shouted. "Why didn't you say it was you!"

"Joe Hardy, how was I supposed to know you were in here?" Iola said. "What did you jump me for? I was trying to save Callie."

"Well, you have. And you've saved us, too," Joe said, as he helped Iola off the floor. They climbed up into the orchestra pit just as the electricity came back on in the theater.

"Iola, did you see the man who knocked into Callie?" Joe asked.

"I didn't see anyone. Let's get out of here," Iola replied.

"We came here to search the theater and rule out once and for all whether Callie misplaced the tiara," Frank said. "Let's do it."

Callie and Iola huddled together as they followed Frank and Joe around the theater. Finally the Hardys satisfied themselves that the tiara was not in the theater. At least not in any of the public spaces of the theater. They'd been unable to get into a few locked rooms, like the front box office and the manager's office. But Callie hadn't taken her tote bag or the tiara into those rooms, so she couldn't have left the tiara in them, either.

An hour later the four friends drove away from the theater feeling more frustrated than ever. The rain had stopped, but the gloom in the van was thicker than any fog.

"Hey, wait a minute," Joe said, slamming on the brakes. "We just searched the entire theater and didn't find a tiara, right?"

"Right. What are you getting at?"

"Why didn't we find the replacement tiara— the one Lyla Spring brought in this morning? It was sitting on top of that big leather prop trunk all day."

"He's right!" Callie said excitedly. "And now it's gone. Do you think someone stole it? Is it a clue you guys can use to solve the case?"

"Yes and no," Frank answered. "Yes, I think the jerk who was just in the theater with us may have stolen it. But it's not enough of a clue to help us solve the case. We still don't know who that guy was."

To confirm their suspicions, the Hardys pulled up to a phone booth and called Lyla at home, waking her up. She told them she hadn't taken the replacement tiara anywhere.

"So what do we do now?" Callie asked. "Shouldn't we tell the police about all this?"

"We will," said Frank. "But I know what our pal

93

Con Riley will say—'Guys, drop by sometime when you aren't so light in the clue department.'"

"We've got to make our own breaks in this case," Joe said.

"How?" asked Iola.

"Okay," Frank said, "here's what I've been thinking. Three people want the tiara. They are Harry Hill, his big customer—whoever that is—and the person who stole it from Callie. Well," Frank went on, "Harry's the only one we know of. If we watch him, maybe we'll learn why the tiara is so important."

The next morning, before driving to the theater, Joe dropped Frank a block from Harry Hill's shop. Frank was to begin their stakeout while Joe transported props for Ravenswood.

Frank had planned to walk past the shop slowly, looking around, then find a place he could watch the door from without being seen. Instead, Frank stopped, and read the handwritten note pasted to the window.

"Closed due to illness in the family."

"I wonder what kind of illness," Frank muttered, and began walking toward the theater.

At eight the following morning, Frank and Joe parked their van across the street and down the block from the Hill Costume Supply Company.

The medium-size brick building, painted white, sat in the middle of a block of other one-story stores.

Harry Hill arrived at nine, and for two hours, Frank and Joe watched him change the display in the large window to the right of his door. When he'd finished, the Hardys grinned at each other. They liked Hill's sense of humor. He had a table in the window. Around it he'd seated three mannequins with cards in their hands. One mannequin wore a shaggy gorilla costume; another wore a knight's chest armor, a catcher's mask, and a Mexican sombrero; the third mannequin wore a vampire costume with a Red Cross T-shirt. Finally Hill had taped a sign to the window: You Never Gamble With Hill's Costumes.

After a while, Joe stared out the window on the passenger side of the van. He was looking at the American Restaurant, across the street from Hill's. "I'd better hustle in there, Frank," Joe said. "There's a crime about to be committed."

"A crime?" Frank said, suddenly concerned.

"Yeah. They sell blueberry muffins, and it'll be a crime if I don't get some soon."

Frank stayed in the van, settling back in the driver's seat, with the radio playing quietly.

Suddenly he sat up straight. Someone had just walked into Harry Hill's shop—and it was someone Frank and Joe knew!

Joe came back with a white bag in one hand and an almost-eaten muffin in the other. "Want a muffin?"

"No." Frank didn't take his eyes off Hill's shop.

"Great," Joe said, reaching into the bag for a second helping.

Frank checked his watch. "He's been in there ten minutes."

"Who?" Joe asked.

"Matt Anglim."

"Matt Anglim went in there? How does he know Harry Hill?" Joe's face turned thoughtful as he kept nibbling on the muffin. "Maybe he's just looking for a costume."

"He doesn't wear one in the play," Frank said. "His character just wears street clothes."

The longer Matt stayed in the shop, the more the brothers' curiosity grew. The ten minutes doubled, then tripled. Joe's muffins were long gone. His suspicions remained.

"Maybe he found Callie's tiara," Joe suggested, although he didn't sound too sure.

"He doesn't even know about the tiara. And if he did know, why wouldn't he give it back to Callie?" Frank replied.

Finally Matt Anglim came out of the shop. He was not carrying anything.

"An hour," Frank said, checking his watch.

"And he certainly didn't pick up a costume," Joe said.

They watched in silence as Matt checked the traffic, crossed the street, and disappeared.

As soon as he was gone, Frank hopped out of the van. "Come on."

Joe didn't know where they were going, but he didn't want to miss it. He followed his brother as Frank checked out the row of stores up and down the quiet street. The American Restaurant, Tan-Your-Hide Tanning Salon, Andy's Sports Pro Shop, the Magazine Rack, and others.

Frank passed them all, heading down the street to a pay phone. He shoved in a quarter and dialed a number.

As soon as someone answered, Frank cupped his hand over the receiver. "Harry? It's Andy over at the Sports Pro Shop," Frank said. "Look, I need a costume for a party tonight, but I'm up to my pecs in customers. Mind coming over and telling me what you've got? Something outrageous. I'll pay whatever it costs."

Frank hung up the phone, and Joe smiled. Then they both watched Harry Hill come out of his shop with a stuffed three-ring binder under his arm and head for the sports shop down the block.

As soon as Harry was out of sight, Frank and Joe hurried to the costume shop.

The door was unlocked and the store empty. Frank set the timer on his watch for three minutes. Hill would probably realize he'd been tricked and

97

be back in four. That gave the brothers one minute to get out of the store, after the timer buzzed.

The front room of the store was packed with racks and racks of costumes. Frank and Joe looked around quietly, then went to the back, to the doorway behind the sales counter that led to a back room.

This was where the costume jewelry was kept. Frank and Joe were looking for one particular rhinestone tiara—but there were a dozen in the back room, along with rhinestone-studded handbags, scepters, crowns, and even a rhinestone-encrusted cane.

Frank looked through the jewelry, then at a well-lit workbench where a sparkling necklace lay with some of its rhinestones removed. There was also some kind of jeweler's tool next to the necklace.

In a desk drawer, Joe found a notebook that listed all of Hill's rentals. "Time?" he called.

"One minute gone," Frank answered.

"I've found Callie's name in the rental book for the costumes she rented the day she bought the tiara, but I don't see any other names around that time," Joe said.

"What about Hill's big client?" Frank said, opening drawers. He found necklaces, rings, and wigs, but not Callie's tiara.

Joe flipped some more pages. "I don't see anyone. Hill's only gets about one customer a month."

Joe dropped the rental book into the drawer and gave the drawer a push. It jammed, still open.

"Let's wrap it up," Frank said.

Joe quickly took out his key ring and used one of the keys to jimmy the side of the drawer until it slid closed. "Bingo," he said. Then he saw the necklace on the workbench. Even with two stones missing, it was a bright eye-catcher.

"Wow. I should have worn my shades," Joe said. He walked over to the bench and picked up the shining necklace.

"Almost time to go," Frank said, still looking for anything that seemed out of place.

"Hey, this thing is heavy," Joe said, balancing the necklace in his hand.

"Keep dreaming," Frank said without looking at his brother. "It's just glass."

"You should lift it."

Frank turned around because his brother sounded so serious. He took a step toward Joe. Was there any way that necklace could be—

*Ding ding!* The sound of the bell over the shop door jingling interrupted Frank's thought. The front door of the shop had been opened!

"Must be Hill back," Frank said, his voice dropping immediately to a whisper.

"Tell him he's too early," Joe whispered back.

The brothers scrambled for a hiding place, ending up stuffed behind a tall metal storage cabinet.

The bell jingled again as the front door closed. Then footsteps slowly slapped along the hardwood floor.

"Oh, no!" Joe whispered to his brother.

He started to bolt from the hiding place, but Frank held him back. "What's wrong with you?"

"I left my keys out there!"

# 11 Hide—and Seek

Frank and Joe squeezed themselves against the wall behind the metal cabinet. They could hear the footsteps shuffling through the shop, heading toward the room where they were hiding. A voice muttered unhappily.

He'll *really* be unhappy if he looks behind this cabinet, Frank thought.

Then the footsteps stopped abruptly, along with the Hardys' breathing. They heard the clatter of keys—Joe's keys!—scraping on the wood desk surface. And then came a jingling as the keys were lifted into the air.

Joe's hands felt cold. He looked at his brother. Footsteps. Coming nearer? They were dead.

No! The footsteps were moving away.

The Hardys let out long, silent breaths. Then they heard the sound of a telephone being picked up.

He's probably calling the police, they each thought.

Joe leaned out from behind the cabinet to hear better. As he did, he saw something behind a curtain on the back wall. He grinned, poked Frank, and pointed.

A door! A back door—and they'd been so busy searching for clues, they'd missed it!

"Jake? It's Harry. I found your keys." Harry Hill laughed. "Bet you were looking everywhere."

There was silence. But the Hardys knew what Jake had to be saying on the other end. They stepped out from behind the cabinet and tiptoed toward the back wall.

"What do you mean they're not yours!" Hill shouted. "Hold on a minute."

The phone hit the counter—hard. The footsteps were coming back—fast.

Frank gave his brother a push. They ran out the back door and didn't look back.

"Guess we'll have to walk back home," Joe said as they hurried down the street.

"Guess again." Frank reached into his pocket and pulled out a set of keys, which he jingled in the air.

"Give me a break," Joe said. "I don't want to hear that sound ever again."

The next morning the Hardys were up early. It was Friday—opening night for the play.

Ravenswood had called a dress rehearsal for early afternoon, but Frank and Joe weren't sure they'd make it. They knew they'd take some heat if they missed the rehearsal, but they had to drive to New York City. Their father had set up an appointment for them to talk to a friend of his, someone with inside information.

Fenton Hardy's friend Marty Tauber was the owner of Tauber's Diamond Exchange. If the necklace Frank and Joe had seen in Hill's back room the day before was real, Marty Tauber might be able to help them prove it. He promised their father he'd answer all their questions about the jewelry business, adding "I'll even show them a diamond as big as their tonsils. See if I don't."

"Want to hear something strange?" Joe said as he drove along the highway, checking his outside mirrors left and right. "We're being followed—that guy on the motorcycle."

Motorcycle? That rang a bell with Frank—a loud one. The guy who'd burgled Callie's house had gotten away on a motorcycle. But no one had gotten a good look at the bike or the rider.

Frank leaned over to check the mirror outside his window. A guy riding a big red bike was sticking close to them.

"Can't see his face." Frank stared in annoyance at the smoky visor that hid the rider's features. "Slow down."

Joe lifted his foot off the accelerator. "He's got

brakes, too," Joe said, seeing the biker fall back.
Joe stepped on the gas, but the biker stayed with
them. They couldn't lose him, and they couldn't
get close enough to make an ID.

Once in New York, there was no way Joe could
shake the guy in the dense city traffic. At a long
stoplight, Frank suddenly jumped from the van
and ran back through traffic toward the bike.

Seeing Frank closing in on him, the biker revved
his engine, made a U-turn, and took off in the
other direction. Frank ran through the traffic as
fast as he could, practically climbing over the
hoods of the cars waiting for the light to change.
But he still didn't get a look at the bike's license.

"Want to guess why we're being followed?"
Frank said when he climbed back into the van.

"Because we're so cute?" answered Joe.

Frank rolled his eyes. "Just do the driving," he
said with a laugh.

They parked in a public garage and walked
down the street New Yorkers call Sixth Avenue but
which is officially named the Avenue of the
Americas. Using the plate-glass windows on the
ground floors of the office buildings as mirrors,
the Hardys tried to see if they were still being
followed. But the crowds behind them were too
thick.

Turning down West Forty-seventh Street, they
entered the New York diamond district: a block-

long string of stores and a gridlock jumble of pedestrians. There were older men in baggy suits, lean young men in Italian suits, men in black suits, with black hats and bushy beards. There were women in trench coats and tourists with cameras around their necks. And everyone was interested in the same thing—diamonds. Buying them, selling them, trading them, even stealing them.

Frank and Joe went through the glass doors of a large jewelry store and diamond showroom. All around them people were browsing, staring into display cases of diamond necklaces, rings, earrings, bracelets, and watches. Some of the clerks behind the cases were looking at jewels through a loupe—a small magnifying glass set in an eyepiece. A squint held the loupe in their eyes. Even the customers had their own loupes for examining the gems.

"No wonder they call diamonds ice," Joe said. "I'm getting chills just standing here. These stones must be worth millions."

"What'll it be, fellas?" asked a clerk, a man in a silk shirt with rolled sleeves. "Diamond earrings for your girlfriend? An earring for you?"

"We're looking for Marty Tauber," Frank said.

The clerk's face changed. For some reason that was a very serious thing to say.

"He's expecting us," Joe added.

"Go in that door. If the metal detector says

you're okay, another door will automatically open. Take the stairs one flight up." The clerk pointed with a quick nod of his head.

Security downstairs was tight. But security upstairs was even tighter. No wonder. In these offices, piles of diamonds and other jewels lay around on people's desks. The office at the end of the aisle belonged to Marty Tauber.

He was a big man with a bushy mustache that matched his bushy black-and-gray hair. He wore a bright red tie.

He greeted them standing at a tall wooden desk that came up to his belt and took up much of his small office. "I'm not a sitter," Tauber said, tapping his special desk. "You sit, make yourself comfortable, and you don't run your business well." Out of his pants pocket he pulled a lump of brilliant yellow light about the size of a large peach pit. "An uncut beauty, boys," Tauber said. "A canary diamond."

"Not bad," Joe said.

"Save your allowance," Tauber said. "Save it for about a hundred years and this could be yours." He laughed, tossed the jewel into the air, then put it back in his pocket.

"Mr. Tauber, we saw a tool yesterday where someone was repairing some jewelry," Frank said. "We want to know what it's used for."

The burly man slid open one of the long, shallow drawers in his desk. Inside were all kinds of specialized jeweler's tools. "Find it and show it to me, boys," Tauber said.

It took a minute of sorting through tiny pliers and lightweight hammers to find a tool to match the one they'd seen on Harry Hill's workbench.

"This is it," Joe said, handing Tauber one of the tools.

Tauber shook his head. "Something's wrong," he said. "Either this isn't what you saw, or it wasn't a repair job."

Frank and Joe looked puzzled.

"Boys, these are calipers. They're not used in repairing a setting. They're used for measuring the size of a stone."

Frank looked at the calipers, picturing them sitting next to the rhinestone necklace yesterday.

"What was being repaired?" asked Tauber.

"A necklace. It was a piece of costume jewelry," Frank said.

Suddenly Tauber started laughing. He laughed so hard he'd probably have sat down if there'd been a chair in the room.

"Costume jewelry? You mean paste?" Tauber hooted. "Boys, let's start at one plus one. You don't *repair* costume jewelry. The settings are made from cheap junk that would never stand up to the kind of metalwork real jewelry gets."

"Oh," Frank said, feeling a little confused.

"Believe me, boys. You know what you need to repair a piece like that? A little bottle of glue."

Tauber was getting his chuckles out of this conversation, but Frank and Joe still knew what they'd seen. Frank took a pencil from Marty's desk and started making a sketch on a sheet of paper. It was a quick drawing of the necklace, with the two rhinestones out, that he and Joe had seen on Hill's workbench the day before.

"It looked like this," Frank said, turning his sketch toward Tauber. "Well, sort of. But two of the stones were lying by the calipers. And when Joe picked the necklace up, he said it was heavy."

The word *heavy* caught Tauber's attention enough to glance at the sketch. "Hmmm." He put on a pair of reading glasses, turning the sketch a little this way and a little that way.

Frank thought Tauber was trying to make up his mind about something—and Frank was pretty sure it wasn't whether Frank had talent as an artist. "Does it look familiar, Mr. Tauber?" Frank asked.

"Hmmm," Tauber answered. "Did the stones that were removed," Marty said, pointing at the sketch, "have a clear but bluish cast?"

"We really didn't have a lot of time to look," Joe said, clearing his throat nervously. "Uh, we were sort of just passing through."

"Boys, I don't know what it means, but your sketch looks very much like a famous diamond necklace that was reported stolen from a wealthy Boston widow about a month ago."

Frank and Joe weren't certain what it meant, either. But after their conversation with Tauber, they took the sketch and their thoughts to a small coffee shop around the corner on the Avenue of the Americas.

Frank smoothed the sketch out on the lunch counter as he and his brother sat on swivel stools in the not-so-crowded lunch spot. He wanted to discuss the million possibilities he saw, thanks to Marty Tauber, but the counter waitress, a woman with a long, blond ponytail, paced back and forth right in front of them.

"Well, how about it, guys? What'll you have? What'll it be?" asked the waitress. She leaned her elbows on the counter and looked like she wanted to stay and join their conversation. She stared at the drawing that both boys were studying, and then finally she looked up at Joe. "I think it'll clash with your eyes."

"Root beer," Frank said quickly. Anything to get her to leave.

"Me, too. And a cheeseburger," Joe said.

The waitress went away to put in their order.

"Okay, let's just say that the necklace we saw was the Boston necklace or at least it was real jewels," Frank said. "What does that give us? What were they doing in Hill's shop?"

"Two possibilities—Harry Hill is a jewel thief or he deals in hot jewels," said Joe.

Frank nodded. "But does this have anything to

109

do with Callie's tiara or the break-in at her house?" Frank said.

"It could mean the tiara was real."

"What do you want on it?" the waitress said.

Joe looked up. He wasn't sure if she was talking to him.

"On your cheeseburger," said the waitress, nodding her head. "It'll be my distinct pleasure to bring it to you, but you've got to tell me what you want on it."

Joe smiled at her. "Surprise me," he said.

"Is that a challenge or a threat?" she said. Her hands were poised on her hips.

What was she so mad about? Joe wondered.

"You think just because I'm a waitress serving food to geeks like you and clearing away your dirty dishes that I don't have feelings? You think if I get a paper cut when I open a fresh pack of napkins, my fingers don't bleed?"

Frank looked at his brother. "I love New York," he mumbled.

"Let me tell you something, buster," said the waitress.

Joe swiveled around on his stool and looked out the picture window of the coffee shop. He didn't like to be rude, but he hoped that would shut out the loud and angry waitress.

"Hey, Frank," Joe said, elbowing his brother and pointing outside. "Look who's out there!"

Across the street stood Matt Anglim, leaning in the doorway of an office building.

"What's he doing here?" Joe asked loudly. The waitress was still talking.

"It looks like he's watching us," Frank replied.

"I wonder if he drives a motorcycle." Joe hopped down off his stool.

"Let's ask him," Frank said, following.

"Hey, what's the rush?" asked the waitress. "What about your cheeseburger?"

"I just decided to become a vegetarian," Joe said, leaving money for the food and drinks.

The Hardys ran outside. But the minute Matt saw them, he turned around and began quickly walking down the street.

"Hey, Matt!" Joe called.

Had he heard?

"Matt!"

The Hardys were trying their best to cross the wide Avenue of the Americas. But the street was jammed with taxis, trucks, and buses. And Matt Anglim wasn't walking—he'd taken off at a sprint!

# 12 On Top of the World

New Yorkers move quickly, trying to get *from* somewhere *to* somewhere at top speed. Matt Anglim was moving quickly, too—trying to get *away.* At least, that's what Frank and Joe thought as they saw him take off down the Avenue of the Americas.

He dodged pedestrians, dashed through crosswalks, and cut in front of cars turning corners. And he was making good time—better than the traffic. Finally he cut across Forty-second Street, heading toward Fifth Avenue. As he neared the New York Public Library, with its carved stone lions guarding the steps, Matt slowed to mingle in with the crowd.

"He thinks he's lost us," Joe said. "Let's hang back and see where he goes."

The Hardys kept a safe distance back. They'd already memorized everything Matt was wearing —white high-tops with green stripes, olive military-looking pants, a gray cotton sweater. He'd be easy to find in a crowd.

Matt went up the first level of library steps and looked around. Was he looking for Joe and Frank? He seemed to be trying to look around without looking as if he were doing it. It was always funny when amateurs tried to act like detectives. Matt didn't stay long on the steps to the library. He kept on going down Fifth Avenue, looking back every once in a while.

Finally he crossed Thirty-fourth Street, turned right, and spun through the revolving doors that led into the lobby of the Empire State Building.

Frank and Joe followed him inside. They found him standing in front of the ten-foot-high painted glass murals of the Eight Wonders of the World.

"Hey, Matt," Joe said, coming up to where the college student was standing.

Frank moved in from the other side.

Matt gave them each a do-I-know-you? look.

"I'm Frank and he's Joe. We're in the play with you."

Matt's face changed. "Oh, yeah. I wondered where I'd seen you before," he said.

"Probably at the coffee shop on Sixth Avenue," Joe said.

"Avenue of the Americas," Frank added with a smile.

"You guys were up there? I was just there. I didn't see you," Matt said.

His eyes flipped from brother to brother, checking them out to see if they believed him.

"Call me crazy, but I had the feeling that you were running away from us," Joe said.

Matt laughed. "You guys watch a lot of detective movies or something?" he asked.

Frank nodded and laughed, too. Then he looked serious again. "Did Paul Ravenswood call off the dress rehearsal for today?" he asked.

"It's this afternoon," Matt said. "I was sitting around getting opening-night jitters. So I thought I'd come into the city, do the tourist stuff, maybe relax a bit."

"Yeah, right. So did we," Frank said, before his brother could say anything else. "So—are you going up to the observation tower?"

"Uh, well . . ." Matt hesitated.

"Isn't that what most people come to the Empire State Building to do?" Joe asked. "I mean, why else come in here?"

A tight smile came over Matt's face. "Sure," he said nervously, looking at the sign that read: Elevator to Observation Tower.

Getting to the observation level of the building involved a series of steps. First the three of them rode an escalator down to the ticket booth. Then they rode an escalator up, with admission tickets in their hands. Then they got in line for the elevator.

They stood behind a family with three little kids who screamed with excitement while they pushed and shoved each other. In the elevator, Matt told jokes to the kids, but he kept glancing at the floor indicator as the elevator rose higher and higher. Finally the elevator reached the eightieth floor, and they got off.

The second elevator, which took them from the eightieth floor to the observation level, was a fast, ear-popping ride. Matt moved into a corner and didn't say anything during that trip.

Why was he outside the coffee shop? Joe kept wondering. And what's he getting so nervous about now?

When the elevator emptied out on the one hundred second floor, Matt was the last one off. There were lines of people everywhere—waiting to take the elevator down, waiting to buy souvenirs, probably waiting to get into the rest rooms.

There was even a line waiting to take a third elevator up to the very highest point—the tower. But the biggest crowds were outside, on the semienclosed walkways that surrounded all four sides of the building. From behind safety fences, visitors could look out for miles in every direction.

"It's a clear day. We'll probably be able to see all the way to Bayport," Joe said, moving toward the south walkway. "We might even see Paul Ravenswood pulling his hair out."

"You know what, guys," Matt said, checking his watch and turning back toward the elevator. "It's getting late. I'm going to head back."

Frank and Joe both stared in surprise. Was Matt really going to come all the way up here and then not even look outside?

Matt's face was beaded with sweat. "The truth is, you guys, I'm scared of heights. I don't want to go out there."

"Gee, that's too bad," Joe said. "Frank and I love it here. Why don't you grab something to drink, and we'll be right back."

Joe took his brother's arm before Frank could argue with him. The two of them walked down the steps leading onto the redbrick walk. It was a beautiful clear day that added a fresh sparkle to New York for as far as the eyes could see.

"What's up?" Frank asked. "I don't think we should leave him. He might run. And I wanted to stick close, to see if he was driving a car or a *motorcycle.*"

"Yeah, but are you thinking what I was thinking?" Joe said. "I mean, this guy's stories have more holes than Chet Morton's gym socks."

"For instance?"

"For one—why was he running from us?" Joe

116

asked. "And why did he come to the Empire State Building when he's afraid of high places?"

"I don't know, but we won't find the answers by standing out here. We're only going to get a suntan."

They hurried back inside, fighting against the crowds who were trying to come out.

"So," Frank said when they finally found Matt again near the elevators—he'd taken off his gray cotton sweater and rolled up the sleeves of his light tan shirt—"do you need a ride back to Bayport?"

Before Matt could answer, Joe started pulling on Frank's arm again. "I'll bet the line for the binoculars is really short now."

Frank stared at his brother. "The what?"

"Binoculars," Joe said as if he were teaching his brother a new word. "You know, you drop a quarter in the slot and you can look through those great big silver-colored, high-powered binoculars."

"I know what they are." Frank gave Joe a dirty look. "But I thought we were leaving with Matt now."

"Yeah, but I want to look at something. Come with me. It'll only take a second. Be right back, Matt."

When they got outside Frank was frantic. "Are you nuts? What'd you pull us out here for?"

"To see if you saw what I saw," Joe said.

"Didn't we just have this conversation?"

"The button," Joe said, pointing to Frank's shirt. "There's a button missing on Matt's shirt."

Frank squinted at his brother, interested.

"What kind?"

"It's a brown tortoiseshell button, Frank."

Those were the words Frank wanted to hear.

"You mean like the button I found in Callie's house?" Frank said, getting excited.

Joe nodded.

"So that means Matt Anglim broke into Callie's house. . . . He broke into the theater, too. We know because the crowbar patterns matched."

"Right," Joe agreed.

"He's the one who drove a motorcycle."

"And it was probably him under the sheet, in the theater. He probably did it all! He cut the rope of the fire curtain, made those threatening calls to Callie. It's been him all the time."

"I'm not sure, Joe," Frank said thoughtfully. "I mean Matt hadn't even shown up yet when the fire curtain fell. And what about the tiara? This still doesn't solve who stole Callie's tiara."

"Yeah, but Matt's still a good starting point," Joe said. "Come on."

The brothers rushed back inside and zipped to the elevators where they'd left Matt standing. But they were too late—he was gone. The floor indicator showed the down car was on the ninety-sixth floor. They'd probably just missed him.

"Maybe he guessed what we were thinking," Joe said.

"We've got to get him *and* that shirt, or we can forget about proving he broke into Callie's house," Frank said, tapping the elevator call button until an elevator finally came.

Matt may have been gone, but the Hardys had a good idea of where he was headed. They hurried to the parking lot, picked up their van, and started back for Bayport. It was late anyway—and the curtain on the play was going up at eight.

The ride back from New York seemed to last five times as long, as if Bayport had somehow moved.

"The prop knife that almost stabbed Callie— could Matt have done that, too?" Joe wondered. He was driving, and when he drove it was always easier for him to ask questions than to answer them.

"I don't see how," Frank said. "I mean, he just showed up and started reading the scene with Callie. He didn't have a chance to rig the knife, unless . . ."

"Unless what?"

". . . unless he's working with someone else in the cast!"

Joe was stunned. That suggestion gave him a chill. "If Matt's working with someone else in the cast, he—they—could have done it all—the fog machine, the fire curtain, everything."

Joe glanced in the rearview mirror, flashed his

directionals, and switched lanes to pass a slow-moving car.

"Hey, there's quite a parade behind us," he said. "Four highway patrol cars with lights flashing."

"Maybe the governor is late for a mall opening," Frank said.

With their sirens screaming, the four patrol cars caught up to the Hardys' blue van as if it were standing still. But the police cars didn't scream past the van. Instead they surrounded it.

"What's going on?" Joe asked Frank.

*"Pull to the side of the road."* A cold voice blared the order through a speaker system.

It wasn't a real answer to Joe's question, but he knew he'd hear one soon. He steered the van onto the shoulder as ordered. The four police cars followed, sirens still screaming and lights swirling, while the rest of traffic kept going.

*"Get out of the van. Lie facedown on the ground with your arms and legs spread!"*

Frank and Joe looked at each other in shock. They knew this wasn't any time to argue. The voice blasting from the speaker was dead serious.

The Hardys slowly stepped out from opposite sides of the van. Two patrol cars were parked in front of them, two in back. The sirens had been turned off, but the strobe lights were still blinking, and the radios squawked. The brothers slowly knelt, then lay flat on the ground.

They heard car doors opening, booted feet running toward them.

"Hands behind your back. Now!" shouted a hard voice.

The Hardys couldn't see any of the officers.

Click! Handcuffs had been snapped around their wrists. They felt a strong pull on the cuffs—to make sure they were locked tight. But no one spoke.

"What's this all—" Joe never got a chance to finish his question.

"Which one of you is Frank Hardy?" a voice interrupted.

"I am," Frank said.

"In case you haven't figured it out, you're under arrest—for reckless endangerment, intent to destroy public property, and attempted murder! Read them their rights!"

# 13 Under Arrest

"This is a mistake," Joe Hardy said. He squirmed on the ground, his hands cuffed tightly behind his back. "A *big* mistake."

"I think you've stopped the wrong van." Frank tried to be calm and reasonable. Maybe then the highway patrol cops would realize they'd grabbed the wrong guys. "Destroying property—attempted murder?" Frank said. "You've got to be kidding."

"No, we're not kidding," said one of the officers, still covering the Hardys with his gun. "We'll talk about it after we go over your van."

Frank and Joe were hauled to their feet by their handcuffs and stuffed into the backseat of a patrol car. From there they could see the four highway patrol officers searching every inch of their van, top to bottom, and underneath, too.

"What are they looking for?" Joe asked.

"I don't think it's overdue library books," answered Frank.

Whatever it was the officers expected to find, they didn't find it. But that didn't clear the tension in the air. It only made it worse.

One of the four officers, a tall, thin woman, climbed into the front seat of the patrol car and looked back at the Hardys. She wrote something down on a report form and then took a small, portable tape recorder out of her uniform pocket. "This was recorded in the communications room about half an hour before we picked you up," she said, switching on the recorder.

"Hello, this is Frank Hardy. I'm driving a blue van south on the turnpike. I've got a bomb in my car, and I intend to blow up a tollbooth."

Hearing the tape made Frank furious, but, strangely, also made him relax. "Now I know why you guys had to play so rough," he said.

"We're not looking for you to understand," the officer said without any friendliness. "We want answers. Don't you know that even making that call as a joke is still a serious offense?"

"The joke's on us," Joe said bitterly.

"That's not me on the tape," Frank said.

"Are you Frank Hardy or not?" another officer leaned in the open passenger door.

Frank nodded. "That's my name, but that's not my voice," he said. "If you compare my voiceprint with your tape, they won't match."

"Everyone's a police expert," growled the officer standing by the door.

"You didn't find any explosives in our van, did you?" Joe said. "I'm telling you, we were set up. Do we look like the kind of bozos who like to be picked up by the police?"

The officer in the front seat looked back and forth from Joe to Frank, as if she were watching a slow-motion tennis game. Then she shook her head slightly. "There are lots of people who pull fire alarms just to see the trucks drive up."

"Not us," Joe said.

"I didn't make that call," Frank repeated. But, he thought to himself, I've got an idea who did— Matt Anglim.

"Maybe you did, and maybe not," said the officer. "We won't get it straight out here. You've got to come back to headquarters."

"We get a phone call, don't we?" asked Frank. She nodded.

"Good," Frank said. "Then I want *you* to make it. Call officer Con Riley of the Bayport Police Department, and ask him about Joe and me."

At the station, once the highway patrol officer had Con Riley on the line, he burned up the telephone wires talking about who the Hardys and their father were. As a result, the brothers were immediately released.

Then Frank got on the phone. "Thanks, Con.

124

Joe and I have one more favor to ask. Can you get on the DMV computer and tell me if a guy named Matt Anglim has a registered motorcycle?"

"You need a plate number, Frank?"

"I just need a yes or no," Frank said.

"The answer's yes," said the Bayport cop.

"That's what I thought." Frank nodded his head at his brother. "Thanks a million. And, by the way, Con, if you like mysteries, you ought to check out the play opening at the Grand Theater tonight. Joe and I are in the final scene."

"I'm not much for plays," said Con Riley.

"Oh, well. Thanks again for the help." Frank hung up.

When the Hardys finally arrived at the theater it was just an hour before curtain. But as soon as they joined the cast backstage, they realized the curtain might not go up at all.

Paul Ravenswood was a mess. His shirt could have passed for a washcloth because it was so soaked with sweat. "Matt Anglim didn't show for the dress rehearsal this afternoon, and he isn't here now."

That didn't surprise the Hardys.

"Don't count on him," Joe said.

"Yeah, it's a long story, but Joe and I think that he's been involved with all the trouble around here," Frank added. "He knows now that we're on to him so he's on the run."

"Couldn't you have chased him away *after* the performance?" asked the nervous director. "He was a great actor."

Joe looked over at Iola, wearing her good-luck baseball cap. He grinned, but she seemed to have left her smile at home.

"And I suppose you chased Raleigh Faust away, too?" Paul Ravenswood stepped in front of Joe, demanding an answer.

"Faust hasn't shown?" Joe asked.

"I know where he is, darling," said Amelia McGillis. She was wearing stage makeup about an inch thick and wore a flowered kimono. A spotted feather boa was draped around her neck. "He's at the cemetery. Goes there before every performance."

"That's very sentimental." Ravenswood looked as if he were about ready to break down completely. "He probably visits a dear one who's buried there."

"Truth is, darling," said Amelia McGillis knowingly, "Raleigh doesn't have any relatives. He just goes there because it's quiet."

Ravenswood rolled his eyes in misery. He glanced at his watch and then tore it off his arm and threw it across the stage.

"Where's Callie?" Frank asked. "Dressing room?"

Iola shook her head.

"Callie was here, but she must have left. She

126

missed the afternoon dress rehearsal," Lyla Spring told Frank.

"I don't know *why* I agreed to direct this show. It's *killing* me." Ravenswood moaned dramatically.

"Hey, Callie is very dependable," Frank said. "Why would she leave and not come back?"

Iola shrugged.

Paul Ravenswood started pacing again, twisting his hands. "Iola, do you know where your brother is right now?"

"Yes, unfortunately," Iola said. "Right now Chet's sitting out in the audience. He wanted to get a good seat."

"Bring him to me instantly," the director commanded.

Iola waited a second to see if Ravenswood would change his mind. He didn't, so she dashed to get Chet.

On the way, she almost ran into Raleigh Faust. "A gracious evening to you all," he said loudly, giving his voice a strong warm-up, and looking around. "We seem to be missing a few essential characters," he said. Then he saw Iola returning, with Chet right behind her. "What's *he* doing here?"

"Raleigh, darling," said Amelia McGillis, "it's not bad luck to have a visitor backstage."

"It's bad luck to have *him* anywhere in the state," Faust said, moving into the background.

"Hiya, Mr. R. Hey, guys," Chet said.

"Chet," Ravenswood said.

Frank could see that the director was obviously debating whether to put his arm around Chet's shoulder, buddy-style. In the end Ravenswood couldn't bring himself to do it.

"Chet," Ravenswood said again, only more friendly. "There are times when destiny shines a spotlight on a special someone, and sometimes that happens when we least expect it."

"Yeah?" Chet stared at Ravenswood.

"Chet, what I'm trying to say is you'll have to play your part tonight. We need you. You're going out there a nobody, but you're coming back a star."

"More probably he'll go out a nobody and come back as even less," Faust muttered loudly.

"Okay, Mr. R.," Chet said with a shrug. "What part do you want me to play?"

"The killer, of course!" Ravenswood nearly shrieked. "You're the only one who's read the lines before—even if you don't remember them."

"Hey, don't worry. I'll fake something. No problem. You still want me to kill Callie?"

"That won't be possible—Callie isn't here," Paul Ravenswood said. "Lyla, you're Callie's understudy. Have you memorized the play?"

"Well, yes, because you said to. But you don't want me," Lyla said modestly.

"Get dressed and made up," said Ravenswood. "You'll be our homecoming queen tonight!"

"Mr. Ravenswood, I don't know," Lyla said. "Shouldn't we wait? Callie could be here any second."

"Must have been something about that phone call," Raleigh Faust said, mostly to himself.

Frank's ears were on high sensitivity when it came to Callie. "What phone call?" he asked, moving toward the actor quickly.

"Oh, around lunchtime. Let me think," Faust said, dramatically putting his fingers to his forehead as if that would help him remember better. "She got a phone call from Iola."

"Huh?" said Iola.

"I couldn't help overhearing some of the conversation," Faust went on. "Iola must have said she was in big trouble and needed Callie to come help her immediately. Anyway, Callie ran out of here fast."

"Hey, Frank . . . Joe . . . something's wrong. I didn't make that call." Iola's face was pale.

A panicky feeling started to bubble up into Frank's throat. Someone had lured Callie out of the theater—but who? Matt Anglim? Harry Hill? And why? Were they trying to kidnap her? Did they still think she knew something about where the missing tiara was?

Frank and Joe had pulled a lot of the pieces of

this mystery together. But now time had run out. Callie was in danger, the play was about to start, and they didn't have enough evidence.

"I'm going to call in the police, anyway," Frank said, thinking out loud. But before he could move, a piece of scenery hanging in the fly space suddenly slipped and dangled dangerously above the stage.

"Don't worry, Mr. Ravenswood. I'll get it," Lyla said. "Hurry, everyone. Curtain in half an hour, you guys," she called as she scampered up to the catwalk to fix the scenery.

Everyone else moved toward their dressing rooms to get ready. But Frank and Joe stayed behind, watching Lyla.

Suddenly, as if their heads were hooked up to the same brain-wave machine, Frank and Joe each had the same thought.

Lyla!

Who else but Lyla could so easily have gone up in the fly space to cut the rope that sent the fire curtain crashing down near Callie? It couldn't have been Matt Anglim—he was terrified of heights! And almost everyone else had been accounted for immediately after the accident. Only Lyla and Amelia McGillis had been out of sight when it happened.

Frank and Joe exchanged a silent look that only brothers or best friends could understand.

They watched Lyla for a moment more as she

walked confidently across the narrow, shaky cat-walk.

"Are you thinking what I'm thinking?" Joe asked.

Frank nodded.

"Cutting the fire curtain, chemicals in the fog machine, bloodied piano rolls. They're not exactly standard MO for professional jewel thieves," Joe said.

"We've been looking for one guy doing it all—one explanation that would cover everything! But that's where we've been wrong," Frank said. "Harry Hill and maybe Matt, they want to get the tiara back, probably because it has real jewels in it. So Matt broke into Callie's house and the theater looking for the tiara. All of that sounds like basic jewel thief stuff. But someone else has been pulling a different number around here, too . . ." His voice trailed off.

Frank looked grim. "I'll get on the phone, try and track down Callie," he said in a quiet voice. "You go through Lyla's office while she's fixing the scenery. See what you can find. And do it fast. We've still got to find Callie."

Joe left his brother and hurried to Lyla's cramped and crowded office. The silver-framed photo of Lyla's missing sister smiled at Joe. It made him feel funny about what he was going to do. But he did it, anyway. He pushed aside stacks of paperwork, stacks of posters, and piles of scripts. Some of the papers were covered in a thin layer of dust, which had collected even before Lyla had become the Bayport Players' production assistant. Joe looked in drawers and searched the cabinets. He finally found what he was looking for in an old cardboard box, shoved so far back on top of the file cabinet that Joe almost missed seeing it. He had to move two heavy stacks of scripts away to get to the box. When he pulled off the lid, the flash of light reflected from the overhead fixture.

Then he saw it—Callie's exquisite, gleaming diamond tiara!

# 14 A Shot in the Dark

Joe Hardy reached into the cardboard box and picked up the tiara. Not a lightweight. That was enough of a clue to tell him there was something different, something special about it. It sparkled with a deep inner glow.

Who used to wear this? Joe wondered. A queen? A princess? How did Harry Hill get it? And why did Lyla take it? Just to get at Callie? Why? Or did Lyla know the tiara was real?

Joe thought about those questions as he raced back to his brother, the tiara held tightly in his hand.

Frank was still on the phone, calling everyone he knew to see if anyone had seen Callie. Paul Ravenswood, Amelia McGillis, Iola, and Raleigh Faust were standing nearby, in costume, nervously

133

trying to prepare for the play but listening to every word Frank said. Chet Morton was holding a script, but not reading it, and Lyla was just coming down from the catwalk, her face pink from the hard work of hanging the scenery.

"Look what I found," Joe said, coming up with the tiara.

"Hey, cool," Chet said. "That looks like Callie's."

Frank dropped the phone back in its cradle when he saw Joe.

"Where did you find that smashing tiara?" Paul Ravenswood said. "It's perfect."

Joe looked over at Lyla, who suddenly became excited and happy.

"Joe, that's great. Where did you find it? Callie's going to be so glad to see it and . . ."

Joe cut off her phony act. "Stop it, Lyla," he said. "You know where I found it. In your office."

"Well, who put it there?" she said.

"We think you did," said Frank.

Lyla gasped dramatically. "Me?"

"We know you stole the tiara," Frank said. "We just don't know why. Have you really become a jewel thief, Lyla?"

"A jewel thief? You've got to be kidding, Frank," Lyla said.

"I'm dead serious." Frank took the tiara from Joe. "Callie's been in a lot of trouble because of this. This isn't a piece of costume jewelry."

"It's not?" Lyla said, and so did several other people, all talking at once.

"No. We think it's a very valuable hunk of jewelry, made with real diamonds. And real thieves are trying to get it back," Frank said.

"I didn't know that," Lyla said quickly. "I just took it because . . ." She stopped, realizing she'd given herself away.

"Go on, Lyla," Frank said. "Hurry."

"I'm sick of Callie getting all the breaks. I'm an actress, too, you know. I'm good, I've studied, but I'm just not as pretty as she is. You all just take me for granted. 'Lyla will do it. Lyla will fix it.' I figured if Callie quit, I'd get her part—the part I deserve."

"The fog machine, the knife—you did all of it to scare Callie?" asked Joe.

"Yes," Lyla said with a nod.

"But how did you drop the fire curtain and get down from the catwalk without being seen?" Frank asked.

"There's a little doorway up there right off the catwalk. It leads to some dressing rooms that nobody uses anymore."

As Lyla spoke, her hand reached out and touched the tiara. Her fingers traced the surfaces of the larger stones. "So all I had to do was cut the rope when no one was under the curtain, run across the catwalk, squeeze through the door, and run down the stairs. I got out through the wall of the downstairs women's dressing room. Then I zipped down to my office."

"That was you who tried to trap us on the second floor the other night!" Frank realized.

"Yeah, you guys don't scare easily," Lyla said matter-of-factly. "I thought for sure that player-piano gimmick would fry your brains."

Frank was silent for a moment, thinking, trying to get the whole picture for once. Everyone— even Paul Ravenswood—was quiet, waiting to hear what horrible revelation would come out next.

"Let's get it straight. You stole the tiara to freak out Callie, and you set up all those fake 'accidents' to make her quit the play. But you didn't know about the diamonds in the tiara."

"Right," Lyla insisted.

"How about coming to the theater during the storm? Chasing us around wearing a sheet?" Joe said.

"That wasn't me. Honest."

Now it was all becoming clear to Frank and Joe. If the sheeted figure hadn't been Lyla, then it must have been Matt Anglim.

"The only other thing I did was . . ." Lyla stopped.

"What?"

"I made those calls to Callie."

"The voice was a guy's," Joe pointed out.

"No—it was me. I told you. I'm a pretty good

actress," she said sadly. "I can change my voice easily."

"But Callie didn't quit, did she?" Chet Morton jumped into the conversation.

"No," Lyla said bitterly.

Frank stepped around Chet and moved toward Lyla quickly. "So what did you do to her? Where is she?" Frank asked.

Lyla backed away from Frank. "I didn't do anything to her. I just called her up and pretended to be Iola. I told her—I mean, Iola told her—that I was in superdeep trouble and only Callie could help me out. I said, drive to the parking lot of the Big Rainbow store—"

"Which one?" Joe asked.

"Elmhurst," Lyla said.

"That's only ten miles away," Joe said. "Lucky you didn't send her to San Francisco."

"Then what?" Frank asked Lyla.

"I was sobbing and told Callie to sit in her car and wait for me—no matter how long it took me to get there. I knew Callie would do anything for Iola. I'll bet she's still there, waiting."

Frank reached immediately for the telephone, getting the number of the Big Rainbow store. A moment later he was talking to the manager.

"Hello. Could you please check and see if there's a girl sitting in a small orange car with one whitewall and three blackwall tires in your parking lot?" Frank asked.

137

"What's the joke?" said the manager.

"It's no joke. Would you please check?"

"Hey, it's a big parking lot," said the manager.

"This is very, very important," Frank pleaded.

"This better not be a joke." The phone banged down on something.

Frank could hear the ring and clatter of cash registers and sappy, piped-in music.

Finally the store manager was back on the phone. "Okay, the car's out there, kid. And there's a girl in it. Now what's the joke? You got some clever line to yell, then you hang up?"

"Please take a message to the girl. Her name's Callie," Frank said.

"Oh, brother. You kids are something else," said the manager.

"Tell her to come back to the Grand Theater as fast as she can. Tell her Frank Hardy called you. Please, this is very serious."

The manager hung up. Frank hung up, too. "He's no sure bet," he said.

"What do we do now?" Joe asked.

"*You* go get her!" Paul Ravenswood said, coming suddenly to life.

"There isn't time to drive there and back before curtain," Frank said. "We'll have to wait, and hope Callie shows up in time. I know one thing—you're not going on in her place, Lyla."

The girl looked away. "No, I guess not."

"Does that mean no play?" asked Chet.

138

"Absolutely not!" cried Ravenswood. "We'll delay the curtain fifteen minutes, then we'll just have to begin without her. Fortunately, she's not on until the middle of the first act. And what about you two? You don't look like police officers. Costumes, guys—where are your costumes?"

Frank and Joe finally went to the men's dressing room and changed out of their blue jeans and into police blues. By the time they had all their stage makeup on, the play had begun. The Hardys thought about their lines, they thought about the tiara, and they thought about Callie and whether she'd make it to the theater in time.

Then they took one step out of the dressing room and froze.

Standing in the hallway was Callie, holding the dazzling tiara in her hand. She thrust the tiara at Frank. "Here," she said, "I want you two to hang on to this until I need it for the homecoming dance scene." Her voice was gruff, but her eyes thanked Frank—and Joe—for all they'd done.

"Iola helped me get dressed fast," Callie said. "She also filled me in on what's been going on. Lyla told Iola she was really sorry for what she did."

A voice called, "Five minutes, Callie."

It was almost time for her to go onstage.

"Listen, Callie, you've got to make one quick phone call first," Frank said.

After the play the Hardys would have to turn the

tiara over to the police as suspected stolen property. So this was their last chance to prove that Harry Hill and Matt Anglim were jewel thieves. They had to set a trap for Hill, something that would lure him to the theater after the play.

Frank told Callie what he wanted her to do. She picked up the phone and called Harry Hill.

"Mr. Hill? Hi, it's Callie Shaw. I just found it—right, your tiara. I'm going to wear it tonight during the performance, but I'll give it back to you right after that. Okay?"

"What did he say?" Frank asked when Callie had hung up.

"It sounded like *hrrmpffg*," said Callie. "He wasn't happy."

"Callie, come on," Lyla said, waving her arms. "It's almost your cue."

Callie nodded. "I'm ready." Then she looked at Frank. "I don't get it. What's up?"

"We'll see after the play," Frank said. "Hill will either try to steal the tiara then, or he'll let you give it to him."

"Either way, it doesn't matter," Joe said. "Frank called Con Riley and asked him to be here tonight. Hopefully, he'll show. Then I'll fill him in so the police will know what to expect."

They hurried toward the darkened wings, the entrances of the stage. Raleigh Faust was just coming off. Obviously, he'd just been in a scene with Chet, because he was red with rage. "He froze," Faust complained. "He's standing out there, not saying a word. He looks like a statue."

"Break a leg, Callie," Lyla said.

"Haven't you done enough?" Joe snapped.

"That's a good-luck wish in the theater, Joe," Lyla said.

Callie gave Frank a quick smile and followed a few steps behind Raleigh Faust onto the stage. The audience applauded Callie's entrance and then grew quiet to hear her first speech.

"Hello, Mother," Callie said in a clear, loud voice. Instantly she was her character, Diane. "Hello, Neal," she said to Chet, who was just staring at the audience. "Sorry to hear about your laryngitis."

When he saw Callie's friendly face, Chet started to clear his throat. The noise he made sounded like a garbage disposal stuck in high gear. Finally he said something. "Uh, don't worry about my laryngitis, Diane. It could have been worse. I could have lost my voice."

The audience laughed, but backstage Paul Ravenswood dropped to his knees. "Please let them say *some* of the lines as they were written."

"He's about as much like a psychopathic killer as a dog biscuit," Raleigh Faust said, storming off the stage again.

Everyone who wasn't onstage or changing costume stood at the right side of the stage, enjoying the play even though they seldom saw the faces of the actors.

Shortly after the third act began, Callie came out of the dressing room and stopped beside Frank and Joe in the wings. They looked up at her and gasped.

Callie wore a long, white silk formal gown. The dazzling tiara, which Frank had given back to her at the end of the second act, sat on Callie's head as if it belonged there.

"Break a leg," Frank whispered as Callie, hearing her cue, strode onstage and began to speak.

Suddenly Frank and Joe saw two men in ski masks and long raincoats, each running down one of the side aisles. The men leapt to the stage from both sides, trapping Callie and Amelia McGillis between them—and their guns!

Some of the people in the audience, thinking this surprising new event was part of the play, began to laugh and applaud.

The two men pointed their guns right at Callie, who was standing with her mouth wide open in surprise.

"The tiara!" barked one of the men, cocking his gun. "Give us the tiara—now!"

# 15 Tying It Up

For a few horrible seconds, Frank and Joe didn't do anything. Where guns were involved, doing nothing was better than doing the wrong thing, Frank knew.

Con Riley, why aren't you in the theater? Frank thought. He took a deep breath. "Con's not here," Frank whispered to Joe. "He wasn't kidding about not going to plays. So—"

"Maybe he just got delayed," Joe interrupted, "and he's on his way." It was more of a wish than a statement.

". . . so we've got to come up with some plan," Frank continued. "First, someone has to call the police." Frank looked around.

"I'll do it," Lyla said. "I'll use the phone in my office." She slipped quietly away.

Onstage, one of the masked men was closing in

on Callie. She kept backing away, slowly. No sudden movements, no fights, but no cooperation, either. But she was almost out of backing-up room. A few more steps and she would walk into the backdrop of the set.

Frank took a step toward the stage, but Joe pulled him back.

"We just want the tiara and nobody'll get hurt," said the guy with the red ski mask.

Callie silently backed away a little more.

"We've got to do something," Faust said angrily, leaning over Frank's shoulder and peeking on-stage. "I wish I could help. I played a hard-boiled detective once. Maybe . . ."

Suddenly the perfect idea clicked in Joe's head.

"Hey!" Joe said, plucking at Frank's shoulder. "Look at us! We're dressed as police officers. We could *act* like police officers. Let's go."

"Let me remind you," Paul Ravenswood warned. "Your guns are loaded with blanks. They have bullets."

"We only have to keep them busy for a few minutes, until the police get here," Frank said.

"Hold on just a sec," Joe said. "I've got an idea." He ran over to Iola at the board, where she was controlling the lights, and whispered something to her.

"Now, let's do it," Joe said, rejoining Frank and mumbling something to him.

Chet Morton cleared his throat nervously. "I'll stay back here and watch for the police," he said.

Joe and Frank took a deep breath and gave each other a thumbs-up sign for good luck. Then they walked onstage with their blank-loaded guns drawn.

"Police! Freeze! Put down your weapons! We've got the place surrounded," Joe called out.

His heart was pounding. Would the masked men buy it? Or could they tell that Frank and Joe were just two kids who'd gotten themselves in too deep this time? As long as the crooks didn't shoot . . .

"Hey, Jack? How'd they get here so fast?" said the man in the green ski mask. "You said we could hit and git—hello, goodbye, and gone."

"Shut up," said the man in the red ski mask.

The audience laughed and applauded wildly, and Jack yelled, "Shut up—all of you!" But that only made the audience laugh harder.

Then in one quick desperate move, Jack, the man in the red mask, ran over and grabbed the tiara, taking some of Callie's hair with it.

"You asked for it," Joe said. He aimed his gun straight up and fired.

Hearing that signal, Iola killed the lights.

Instantly the stage was in complete darkness. Frank and Joe threw down their prop guns and dove toward the two masked men. It was a risky move, but then their whole plan was risky! The

145

Hardys couldn't see a thing in the dark, but they'd memorized the men's positions.

Frank hit his target in the stomach, and heard a surprised *oooph* as the man had the wind knocked out of him. Joe tackled his victim around the ankles—a favorite Joe Hardy move. It worked! The sound of two guns hitting the wooden stage floor one after the other echoed in the darkened theater!

"Lights, Iola!" Joe shouted.

Immediately the lights came back on. The two masked men were on the stage floor, trying to clear their heads. Frank and Joe jumped to their feet. Where were the guns? Then they saw the answer. Amelia McGillis held both weapons and they were both aimed at the ski-masked men!

"Freeze-frame, darlings," she told the masked men. "A captive audience. I love it."

When he saw that it was over, the man in the green ski mask tore off his mask in disgust and threw it at his partner. "Jerk!" he shouted.

The audience burst into applause at what they thought was the grand finale scene of a very short last act. And to complete the effect, Lyla brought the curtain down right then. The applause was thunderous.

Seconds later, Con Riley and several other *real* police officers arrived. Riley hurried onstage.

"Jewel thieves," Frank said, as Amelia McGillis turned over the guns she was holding to an officer.

"They were after Callie's tiara, which happens to be real and is probably stolen property. And we suspect these guys are part of a jewel-stealing ring."

Con Riley smiled. "This sounds better than any play. Let's clear this place so you guys can tell me more." Riley handcuffed the thieves and read them their rights.

At Con Riley's request, the curtain was raised again, and Paul Ravenswood stepped to the front of the stage. He explained to the audience that what they had just seen had not been part of a play—in fact it was nothing like the play that he wanted to put on. "Instead of entertainment," said the disappointed director, "you witnessed a real attempted robbery."

The audience listened in shocked silence to everything Ravenswood had to say. Then they did a strange thing. They began to applaud again, to whistle and applaud, to cheer and applaud. And they wouldn't stop until Frank and Joe Hardy came out to take a bow.

Early the next morning the cast and crew of *Homecoming Nightmare* gathered in the old Grand Theater to hear an announcement from Paul Ravenswood. Before he could speak, however, everyone insisted that the Hardys tell them what had happened at the police station the night before.

"Do tell all," Raleigh Faust said, stepping closer

to the Hardys. When he realized he was standing beside Chet Morton, he quickly moved back.

Frank started at the beginning, telling the story as it had been revealed during all-night interrogation sessions with the police.

"You've probably guessed that Harry Hill doesn't make his living renting theatrical costumes," he explained.

"Well, last night he finally admitted that he'd been acting as the middleman for stolen jewels. Thieves brought stolen items to Harry. He paid the thieves, broke the jewelry down, and sold the gemstones one by one to other buyers. That's common practice among people who deal in stolen jewelry. Without their settings, the individual gems are hard to identify. And of course no one questioned seeing jewels go in and out of a costume shop. It was a perfect front."

"Sort of a jewelry chop shop," Chet Morton said with a laugh.

"Right," Joe said. "Hill had even told us the truth—about some things. Someone *did* give Callie the wrong tiara. Hill just forgot to mention that it was a real diamond tiara."

"And that customer Hill was talking about?" asked Faust.

"The customer was real," Joe said. "Real angry —he'd already paid for the diamonds, and Hill couldn't deliver them. So he was putting Hill under a lot of pressure to get them back."

"That's where Matt Anglim came in," Frank said. "The police picked him up at his parents' house last night."

"Darling, how did a nice duck like him go swimming in this quicksand?" said Amelia McGillis. "I always liked him."

"He's Harry Hill's nephew," Frank said. "And Uncle Harry promised Matt a bundle of money if he could find the missing tiara. First Matt tried breaking into Callie's house. Then, the same night, he broke into the theater, with no luck. Finally he hit on the idea of joining the play as a way of getting closer to the tiara."

"Fortunately for Matt, Chet made joining the cast very easy," Joe said, giving his friend a pat on the back.

"Helpful is my middle name," said Chet Morton.

Iola pretended to gag.

Frank laughed and continued the story. "The first day Matt rehearsed with us was the day Lyla brought in the replacement. He saw it on the prop trunk and thought Callie had found the lost tiara. So during the rainstorm that night, he broke into the theater again. And this time he got away with a tiara."

"But it was the wrong one," Lyla added, standing off by herself. "It was the one I'd tried to give Callie to substitute for the one I'd taken." The last words didn't come as easily as the first. But she'd said them, and it seemed that people were in a forgiving mood.

"After Joe and I paid a visit to Hill's shop, he suspected we were on to him," Frank went on. "So he put Matt on our tail."

"But Matt blew it when he followed us to New York City," Joe said. "I mean, there was no good reason for it. And then, when we realized that the button we'd found in Callie's house was his, we had him nailed. He must have realized something was up—he tried to get us arrested, figuring it would give him more time to get away."

"You know, you guys can't act your way out of a paper bag," Raleigh Faust said, beaming as if he were complimenting the Hardys. "But you sure can solve mysteries."

It was then that Paul Ravenswood took over the spotlight.

"All right, that's enough about their accomplishments," he began. "Time to get to the real purpose of this meeting. I have an announcement to make. Last night did not go as well as I had planned."

"I don't know, darling," Amelia McGillis corrected her director. "These two kids got a ten-minute round of applause for bagging those jewel thieves."

"Yes, yes, I know," Ravenswood said, with a wave of his hand. "But remember. In the process they also ruined the Bayport Players' chance to get free costumes for a year from Hill's Costume Supply Company."

Which came first, Joe wondered, Paul Ravenswood or the one-track mind? It was a tough question to answer.

"I'm talking about the play, the play we did *not* perform last night," the director continued. "We worked very hard in rehearsal." Ravenswood's eyes noticed Chet. "Most of us anyway," he added. "And I know that you have a play inside you that wants to come out for the audiences in Bayport. That's why I rescheduled our opening performance for tonight! Be back here by seven o'clock sharp!"

Frank and Joe were a little surprised, but Callie looked pleased. And why not? She deserved a chance to play her part all the way through.

After being dismissed by Ravenswood, Callie, Iola, Chet, and the Hardys walked out of the theater into the sunshine of a summer morning.

"Let's go to the park," Frank said.

"Can't," Chet said quickly. "Gotta get ready for the play tonight."

"We could head down to the beach," Joe said.

"Sounds good to me," Frank agreed.

Chet shook his head. "No way. Gotta get ready for tonight."

"I'm impressed," Frank said. "You're really serious about learning your lines for tonight, aren't you?"

151

"My lines? Nah," Chet said. "I've got to finish my costume."

"Costume?" Joe said. "Get real, Chet. Your character doesn't have a costume."

"Oh, yes, he does," Chet said. "Paul Ravenswood doesn't know it, but I'm going to pay him back for all of his yelling and bullying. Tonight the killer is going to be played by a six-foot, two-hundred-pound hot dog!"

At first, Frank and Joe thought he was kidding. But this was Chet Morton. He was dead serious!

"Forget the costume," Frank said with a wink to Joe. "You won't be needing it."

"Why not?"

"Because, Chet," Frank and Joe said in unison, "you're the only guy we know who doesn't need a costume to play a hot dog!"

# NANCY DREW® MYSTERY STORIES
## By Carolyn Keene

| | ORDER NO. | PRICE | QUANTITY |
|---|---|---|---|
| THE TRIPLE HOAX—#57 | 64278 | $3.50 | |
| THE FLYING SAUCER MYSTERY—#58 | 65796 | $3.50 | |
| THE SECRET IN THE OLD LACE—#59 | 63822 | $3.50 | |
| THE GREEK SYMBOL MYSTERY—#60 | 67457 | $3.50 | |
| THE SWAMI'S RING—#61 | 62467 | $3.50 | |
| THE KACHINA DOLL MYSTERY—#62 | 67220 | $3.50 | |
| THE TWIN DILEMMA—#63 | 67301 | $3.50 | |
| CAPTIVE WITNESS—#64 | 62469 | $3.50 | |
| MYSTERY OF THE WINGED LION—#65 | 62681 | $3.50 | |
| RACE AGAINST TIME—#66 | 62476 | $3.50 | |
| THE SINISTER OMEN—#67 | 62471 | $3.50 | |
| THE ELUSIVE HEIRESS—#68 | 62478 | $3.50 | |
| CLUE IN THE ANCIENT DISGUISE—#69 | 64279 | $3.50 | |
| THE BROKEN ANCHOR—#70 | 62481 | $3.50 | |
| THE SILVER COBWEB—#71 | 62470 | $3.50 | |
| THE HAUNTED CAROUSEL—#72 | 66227 | $3.50 | |
| ENEMY MATCH—#73 | 64283 | $3.50 | |
| MYSTERIOUS IMAGE—#74 | 64284 | $3.50 | |
| THE EMERALD-EYED CAT MYSTERY—#75 | 64282 | $3.50 | |
| THE ESKIMO'S SECRET—#76 | 62468 | $3.50 | |
| THE BLUEBEARD ROOM—#77 | 66857 | $3.50 | |
| THE PHANTOM OF VENICE—#78 | 66230 | $3.50 | |
| THE DOUBLE HORROR OF FENLEY PLACE—#79 | 64387 | $3.50 | |
| THE CASE OF THE DISAPPEARING DIAMONDS—#80 | 64896 | $3.50 | |
| MARDI GRAS MYSTERY—#81 | 64961 | $3.50 | |
| THE CLUE IN THE CAMERA—#82 | 64962 | $3.50 | |
| THE CASE OF THE VANISHING VEIL—#83 | 63413 | $3.50 | |
| THE JOKER'S REVENGE—#84 | 63426 | $3.50 | |
| THE SECRET OF SHADY GLEN—#85 | 63416 | $3.50 | |
| THE MYSTERY OF MISTY CANYON—#86 | 63417 | $3.50 | |
| THE CASE OF THE RISING STARS—#87 | 66312 | $3.50 | |
| THE SEARCH FOR CINDY AUSTIN—#88 | 66313 | $3.50 | |
| THE CASE OF THE DISAPPEARING DEEJAY—#89 | 66314 | $3.50 | |
| THE PUZZLE AT PINEVIEW SCHOOL—#90 | 66315 | $3.95 | |
| NANCY DREW® GHOST STORIES—#1 | 46468 | $3.50 | |

and don't forget...THE HARDY BOYS® Now available in paperback

---

**Simon & Schuster, Mail Order Dept. ND5**
200 Old Tappan Road, Old Tappan, NJ 07675
Please send me copies of the books checked. (If not completely satisfied, return for full refund in 14 days.)

☐ Enclosed full amount per copy with this coupon (Send check or money order only.)
Please be sure to include proper postage and handling:
95¢—first copy
50¢—each additonal copy ordered.

☐ If order is for $10.00 or more, you may charge to one of the following accounts:
☐ Mastercard ☐ Visa

Name _____ Credit Card No. _____

Address _____

City _____ Card Expiration Date _____

State _____ Zip _____ Signature _____

Books listed are also available at your local bookstore. Prices are subject to change without notice.          NDD-17